The One Bed Rule

The One Bed Rule

RACHEL LABERGE

Playlist

Adore You | Harry Styles
Something About You | Eyedress
So It Goes | Taylor Swift
Secret | Ann Marie & YK Osiris
Roslyn | Bon Iver & St Vincent
Sweet Disposition | The Temper Trap
Panic | Name Taken
Wildest Dreams | Taylor Swift
I.O.U. One Galaxy | The Ataris
Kiss It Better | Rihanna

For anyone wishing they could pause this timeline and get stormed in with someone like Seth or Claire—this one's for you.

LETTER FROM THE AUTHOR

If you're someone who loves to go into a book blind... turn the page. Don't need content warnings? Get out of here. Flip the page.

It's your last chance.

THE ONE BED RULE is a spicy novella where both characters are truly having a great time. There's not many things to call out in regards to content warnings, but I always want to be as transparent as possible. In THE ONE BED RULE, there's mention of a fatal car accident, and scenes depicting depression, anxiety, and panic attacks.

THE ONE BED RULE is meant for readers 18+, including full sex scenes and mature language.

ONE

Claire

THIS ISN'T WHAT OCTOBER is supposed to feel like. Thanks to the Miami heat, sweat beads on my forehead as I wait for my plane to begin boarding. I can't believe people live in a place where there are no fall leaves or the whisper of a chill in the air. I make a mental note to cross southern Florida off my "places I could live" list. A warm coffee cup between my hands isn't doing me any favors as I feel a drip of sweat make its way down my shoulder blades, but I can't help it: I'm a cappuccino fiend.

Typically I'd be on a private plane, not waiting to board a commercial flight, but Willow—my favorite client and one of the most famous pop stars on the planet—decided to make a quick trip to Italy. There's a piano she wants to look at, so she'll go to her home on the Amalfi coast for a few days and I'll count down the minutes until I'm back in New York.

"Tell me that isn't hot coffee," a gruff voice says with a playful bump into my shoulders.

Seth.

I offer a shrug—he already knew the answer. We haven't spent a ton of one-on-one time together but it's common knowledge I only drink hot coffee. I reply, "Surprised to see you here. How'd Willow manage that?"

"She's got one of my best guys with her and another contact on the ground in Italy. Per her request, I'm going back to the city." The head of my client's security detail rolls his eyes with his *back to the city* comment.

Just like everyone knows I drink hot cappuccinos all year round, we all know how serious Seth takes his job with Willow. He treats her like she's legitimately a part of his family and always feels best in a hands-on role when it comes to Willow's safety.

We've worked together for a while, but that mostly means I'm following the plans he and his team give us—like we did for this award show last night in Miami. I've heard nothing but good things about Seth, but I don't know a ton about him.

"Boarding pass?" I ask, wanting to see where he's sitting on the plane. He squints while handing me a meticulously and evenly folded piece of paper. I open it to see he's in the almost very last row.

This just won't do.

I walk to the desk, ready to work my gate agent magic. While they check what's available, I glance at a group of women to my right. It's clear they're talking about Seth as they try to covertly get a picture of him, which he picks up on immediately—security detail 101. When I look over my shoulder, I see Seth wave to the women and the chorus of sighs and giggles that follow are adorable.

"You're all set, Miss Benton. Here are two new boarding passes for you," the agent says, giving me a smile and a wink.

Satisfied, I walk back to Seth, handing over his new boarding pass.

He whistles. "First Class? Wow."

"Next to me. That's the only downfall," I say, poking fun at myself while taking a long drink of my coffee.

"Stop," he protests, tipping his head. His hazel eyes have flecks of green and brown, and remind me of the autumn leaves I'm missing back home. I've never noticed how pretty they were.

What else haven't I noticed?

Seth is getting something out of his black backpack while I take him in. His dark hair has the start of curls—it's longer than I've ever seen—and it's almost black but peppered with gray. Why is it that men get to age and legitimately get hotter with each year that passes, while the rest of us are out here fighting for our lives? His back muscles ripple as he zips the bag up, lifting up and putting it back on his shoulders—he's wearing a bougie athleisure top with fabric that looks like butter.

Why am I thinking about putting my hands on him? Running my fingers down those muscles on each side of his spine, his shoulders? Fuck, it's been too long. Might need to plead temporary insanity and get back on a dating app, which is code for I need to get laid.

As we board, my phone buzzes: a reminder for my spa day tomorrow morning. The one I've had scheduled for months. We're talking an entire day of being pampered, massaged, and primped.

My muscles relax at the thought of it—the memory from last year. This year, I've really rounded out the experience with a private chef coming to my place to cook me one of my favorite meals.

We're getting settled, me in the window seat and Seth right next to me, when the flight attendant approaches us.

"First, we've got champagne for both of you. And Miss Benton, we've got something a little extra." He hands me a gift, a white bow on a dark brown wrapped box which feels like velvet on my hands. "Truffles for you. Happy birthday and thanks for flying with us."

Shit.

Seth slowly turns and when I look at him, his eyes are wide, all hazel and gorgeous. "Birthday? Is today your birthday, Claire?"

"Yes," I admit, covering my eyes. I don't know why, but this is something I've never really celebrated.

Who am I kidding—I know exactly why I don't like this day. My whole life, my parents were too busy working to ever really plan anything. And then, when I was able to take care of myself in the most basic of ways, they were too busy drinking and pretending I didn't exist. I've always been too independent, desperate for control, because I simply had to. I went no contact with my parents long before it was a hot topic in therapy.

"And what year are we celebrating?" Seth asks, lifting his champagne flute.

I do the same with my flute and say, "Thirty-eight."

"Damn. Didn't think I was an entire decade older than you." He acts like it's some sort of embarrassing fact but it feels like all a ruse. Clearly, the man is still ridiculously hot.

Ten years would make him forty-eight. I actually had no idea how old he was—never really gave it much thought. Looking closer, I see some laugh lines around his eyes when he turns to me, smiling as he says, "Well, here's to you. Happy birthday."

Our glasses clink and we take a sip—the bubbles fresh and bright on my tongue. Fuck, I love champagne.

To be honest, I kind of love how Seth is looking at me right now, too.

Two
Seth

THIS IS ONE OF the worst flights I've ever been on. Thought the whole getting upgraded and sitting next to someone I know, champagne in hand, was supposed to indicate this was going to be enjoyable. *Scratch that.* The seatbelt sign has been on the entire flight, attendants are still buckled into their seats, as turbulence has the plane shaking and dipping while we fly through it. It's been almost two hours and even my stomach is starting to hurt, despite motion sickness never being something I've had a problem with.

Looking over to Claire, she's gripping the arm rest, her knuckles white.

A voice sounds over the intercom. "This is your captain here. Ugh, you can see that the flight path has been rough. In all transparency, a random snow storm is the culprit."

"Snow storm? It's early October," Claire moans to no one in particular.

The captain's voice crackles again. "To keep everyone safe, we're making an emergency landing. We're waiting to get the greenlight from a few small airports in the Carolinas." Before I can even contemplate what the hell that means, there's a significant drop and someone lets out a tiny scream in surprise. Like a reflex, I reach for Claire's hand, holding it tightly in mine.

She doesn't flinch but remains staring forward. A few seconds later, there's another drop, and she's squeezing her eyes shut. Her chest rises and falls in quick motions and it's clear she's struggling.

"It's okay. We're going to be okay," I quietly reassure, leaning closer to her.

She nods but keeps her eyes closed.

"Do you want to talk or do you want to sit in silence until we've landed?" I pose the question.

Claire turns to me, face as pale as her knuckles were a second ago. "Talk. Considering this is the last time we might be able to." We hit another rough patch and her head goes to the left with the momentum.

I reach my other hand over and hold her forearm, drawing circles. "This is not the last time. I've been on much worse flights—"

"Don't tell me about them. Now is not the time."

"When you were a kid, what job did you want?"

She takes a short breath, sighing it out before turning to me, struggling to turn her attention from the unplanned chaos around us. "I wanted to be a teacher. Because of my fourth grade teacher, Mrs. Rivard." Her eyes find mine; outside of the panic and stress, I can see they're chocolate brown. "She was the person who showed me what it was to be seen. Be paid attention to. My parents sucked but that's going to have to be a later story." She practically runs out of breath.

Fuck. That stings. I don't push her on the topic and instead answer it for myself.

"I wanted to be a firefighter and that was actually what I did before this."

"You were a firefighter?"

I nod and she rolls her eyes before looking outside the window—nothing but white from the clouds we're still going through.

The laugh escapes before I can hold it back, "What's that look for?"

"You *would* be a firefighter. That explains the muscles."

"Checking out my muscles, huh?" I wink at her, thankful for the quick joke.

"You wish, Seth. No. I see people and notice their shape like a normal human. Sue me." She makes a circling gesture with the hand I'm not holding and says, "Next question."

We're interrupted when captain comes back over the intercom, "We've got clearance to land in Ridgeview, North Carolina." We look at each other, both shrugging because we've never heard of it. "Hate to tell you that it's going to get a little worse on the descent, but I'd like you to be prepared."

We sit in silence together, both of my hands touching Claire's, trying to help her relax any way I can. There's someone crying in the back of the plane and a kid, probably about eight, who keeps laughing and yelling "Woah!" when there's a bump or drop.

When the plane finally lands, skidding a bit from the ice, it's like there's a collective sigh being let out. And for the first time in my entire life, I clap for the pilot. Claire enthusiastically joins in before pressing herself back into the seat, a spot of sweat broken out on her chest near her collarbone.

"Well, at least this will be a birthday you won't forget," I shrug.

She turns slowly, her eyes like daggers, and I mouth 'kidding'.

And it may not be my birthday, but this is certainly a day *I'll* never forget.

THREE

Claire

"THIS IS A DISASTER," I groan, pacing the hall of the smallest airport I've ever been in. There's a single baggage carousel and a vending machine. If there's something I despise with every cell in my body, it's when my plans fall through. The feeling of being at the mercy of someone else, even if that's Mother Nature, is something that turns my stomach.

"Not fucking ideal, that's for sure. But I'm kind of glad I don't have to get back in the air today," Seth agrees, pressing a hand to his chest. "Good news, though, we got the last rental car." He dangles a set of keys in front of me.

All the flights are grounded for this airport, not that many must come and go, but across this entire region. That's what an October blizzard will do for you. I'm on hold for the last place a Google search brought up as far as somewhere to stay. I hand Seth the phone so I can fill up my water bottle and am amazed at how many people are in this tiny airport. Makes sense, considering it's the entire plane trying to get to New York.

I take a long drink from my bottle, trying to calm my nerves. It feels like my skin is raw—that flight took everything out of me. It's not that I'm a bad flyer, but I absolutely hate when something is a surprise like this—so my first emergency landing is something I could've done without.

Seth waves me over and announces, "They've got a room for us. The Fable Inn. We should get on the road."

I open my maps app, clear my throat and ask, "Any chance we could make the drive?" My screen shows an eight hour drive time. "I've got these birthday plans and..." My voice trails off, because it sounds more pathetic than I typically like to be in front of others.

He takes my phone, crinkling his brows and does his best to consider it. His eyes look to the window and mine follow. It's nothing but a white out. My stomach flips, anxiety pulling at me. If there's something that makes me wildly uneasy, it's driving in the snow. Luckily, I live in a city where most of it is walkable; if not, there's the subway, the bus, and car services.

"I mean, it looks pretty bad. But, let's get on the road and see how it is." His face is soft which makes me even more pathetic for worrying about my birthday. It's just another day. No big deal.

"I'll drive. If that's okay with you?" Seth asks and I feel my shoulders relax.

"More than okay. Thank you," I reply, reaching for my phone. My fingers touch his palm and part of me just wants to latch on. He takes both our bags, wheeling the luggage, and I quickly do my best to keep up with him but I'm wearing Louboutin heels, Chanel slacks, and a matching tailored vest with nothing but my favorite lacy bra underneath. I thought I'd be getting off a plane and headed straight to the city for some random shopping, not getting stuck in some *other* random city.

When we reach the automatic doors leading outside to the rental cars, Seth stops. He takes off his backpack and then his top.

"What the hell are you doing?" I ask, looking around, as people passing by give him the same look I am.

He hands it to me, now wearing only a fitted black shirt. "Here."

When I don't take it, he insists, "You're literally wearing that little vest thing. Your arms are bare. It's a blizzard. Put the shirt on." His voice is gruff and it's a tone I've heard before. It's his I want you to do this thing but I'm not going to really get after you, yet... but it's coming.

I've been through enough today, the energy to push back left about thirty minutes into the flight—one I'm planning to forget. I take the shirt and pull it on. The fabric is soft and warm, smelling like eucalyptus and peppermint.

The doors open and the air rushes forward, stealing my breath. The wind whips flakes of snow that actually feel like tiny icicles against my cheeks. It only takes a few seconds for me to realize Seth was definitely right and the thought of me out here without his shirt makes me feel like an idiot. I don't need to tell him that, though.

Wrapping my arms around myself, doing anything to block the cold, I keep my chin down and look up enough to see Seth. He struggles to pull the roller bags; the wheels are like little snowballs and if I didn't see this with my own eyes, it'd be hard to believe. Weather like this out of nowhere? Put it on a list of things I hate.

Seth finds the rental car, which is ideal considering I can barely keep my eyes open as the wind howls through the parking lot. He opens my door before briefly getting in himself, starts the car and cranks the heat, then gets out again to put our bags in the trunk. I practically leap into my seat, rubbing my hands together in front of the vents which are still blowing cold air, but somehow feel warmer than outside.

When he's situated—his phone connected to the navigation showing our twenty-three minute drive to where we're staying—Seth looks over at me, cheeks red from the winter air. "You ready?"

Hardly. But instead of telling him the truth, I offer a smile and he pulls out of the parking lot.

FOUR

Seth

THIS IS FUCKING BRUTAL. Our crossover SUV crawls at twenty-seven miles per hour as I feel the stress radiate from Claire in the passenger seat. One hand grips the seatbelt clip and the other holds her phone on top of her leg—her knuckles as white as the world outside the window. The only sounds are the swish of the windshield wipers and the whooshing of the air vents—I was playing music, but Claire turned it off a few minutes ago.

She's not okay. To be honest, I hate this too. There was a piece of me that was holding out hope that once we got on the road, we'd be able to consider driving to New York, or at least to a major city in hopes of getting on a new flight sooner than this rinky dink airport we left behind. That piece of me has been stepped on, squashed, and buried beneath a whole pile of snow.

We've been driving for almost twenty minutes and have only made it four miles. We're still probably almost an hour out, I think, as another car spins out ahead of us. Claire sucks in a breath and my hands squeeze the steering wheel even tighter than before.

"So, I'd like to make the call that we don't try to drive back. We stay here, at least for the night, and reevaluate in the morning," I suggest, knowing there's no way we'd make it at this rate.

She slowly nods and then looks at something on her phone.

A few seconds later, her voice is almost a whisper, like she's talking to herself. "I don't have service. Can't even check the weather."

I try to keep my own worry buried deep, in a place Claire could never find it, but this is another reason to try and get somewhere for the night. Us being stranded out here? At night? No thanks.

Hiding my concern from Claire is easy. My job is to think about, plan for, and encounter some of the most dangerous or off-the-wall situations, all while keeping my cool. It's one of the things I've kept with me from my firefighter days, no matter how long it's been.

Fifteen years. That's how long.

The wave of dread threatens to rush through me, but thankfully there's no room with all the existing stress from the drive.

Claire loosens her grip, giving her knuckles a bit of a break, and rubs her upper arms.

"Cold?" I ask as my fingers hover above the temperature controls on the steering wheel.

"No. Not really. I can't stop shivering though," she answers, rolling her shoulders back, and then stretching her neck while still rubbing her arms.

"It's the adrenaline. Not to be this person but try to relax. Do some deep breathing," I suggest. Unfortunately, my words escape me as our car drifts just enough to make her eyes go wide, before the tires grab the road and I'm back in control.

She looks at me and I can feel her eyes, even though I need every ounce of attention to keep us safe. "How can I relax?" Her voice climbs at the end and we might be in meltdown territory. "We're on a fucking ice rink in North Carolina in a car that isn't meant to skate!"

Wouldn't blame her. We've been through it.

"I'm going to keep us safe. I've driven in snow like this before." I tell the tiniest white lie, justifying it with the fact that her stress is creeping into my bones. "Why don't you recline the seat and close your eyes, sleep if you can?" It's not that I haven't driven in the snow, it's just a trigger and one I do anything to avoid.

Claire says nothing but I hear the hum of the seat going back mixed with her slow breathing. I make sure to unclench my jaw and keep my eyes on the road.

"You made it!"

A cheerful, almost sunshiney voice greets us as soon as we rush into The Fable Inn. I've never been more thankful to be inside, off the roads, and out of the air. Fuck. I need a long hot shower.

"Barely," I huff as we walk to the front desk of the small inn. The woman behind the desk—Jess, according to her name tag boasting a little book in the corner—smiles as she leans over to catch a glimpse of the outside.

I'm just fucking thrilled to not be behind the wheel anymore.

She claps her hands, loudly, and Claire jumps. "We're so excited to have you tonight. You're the only guests. Currently, we only have two rooms available, working on some water damage on the other side." She looks past us, down the hallway where the rooms probably are.

Part of me wonders if asking for separate rooms is the move. Maybe we'd both be more comfortable in our own space?

"Good thing, because I hate to tell you, but the power's been going in and out. This is an old building and we haven't done our winter prep yet."

Jess could tell me that I had to sleep in a closet and I'd still be thankful. My capacity for dealing with stress and uncomfortable situations is pretty high—not much bothers me—but I am tapped after today.

"Is there anyway we could get both rooms? If they're available?" While I'm asking the question, Jess' face sort of falls and the brightness dims.

Rubbing her hands today, she says, "Well, I was going to stay in the other room. Given the weather, but if you want—"

"No, absolutely not. We'll be fine with one room," I look to Claire, who smiles and agrees with me. There's a tiny piece of excitement, followed by nervousness, when I think about sharing a room with her.

Jess, relieved she'll have a room, says, "This is The Fable Inn, welcome! The building's kind of split into two, old wiring and all that, so the other side actually has no power. Glad it's the water damaged rooms and not the other two. And, if the power goes out on this side, we have a generator that will kick on. Don't worry about it."

Looking over at Claire, she uses the front desk to hold herself up. My shirt hangs on her a bit and I look down to see her heels covered in snow, some of it clearly touching her bare skin. Jess talks about where The Fable Inn got its name—she's gushing about the library they've built and how it's one of the key pulls to people making the trip.

I don't have the heart to tell her this could be a shack off the road and I'd be happy to be away from the wheel. We'd make it work after the travel day from hell.

Jess continues, "We've got a full kitchen with a ton of ingredients. Feel free to help yourself like it's your own home. Our cook couldn't stay, but he did make a pot of soup and fresh bread." She leads us past the kitchen and my mouth waters at the thought of food. In our rush at the airport, we didn't even think about stopping to eat.

We reach our room and Jess clicks a key in the lock, swinging the door open. "Here's your key. Help yourself to anything you need. Snack basket is on the table for you, water and a few beverages are in the mini fridge. The lounge downstairs has some books, board games. There's an espresso machine at your disposal if you know how to work it." Jess laughs, shrugging her shoulders, clearly letting us know she wouldn't know what to do with it.

Damn. This might not be so bad. Hopefully we can just stay tonight and get back to the city tomorrow, but this will definitely work. I roll our luggage over to a closet, where gray fluffy robes hang.

"Extra pillows and blankets in there." Jess points to the closet and rubs her arms with her hands. "Like I said, this place isn't winterized yet and the wind is fierce. It's going to be cooler in here tonight than I'd like." She looks around the room, which is honestly pretty charming; now that she mentions it, it's not all that warm. Rubbing her hands together, she asks, "Anything I can do for you?"

"Do you by chance have any wine?" Claire asks, a worn smile on her lips.

Five

Claire

I drink my first glass of champagne way too fast as I sit back on the bed. I'm still wearing Seth's shirt over my outfit, and typically I'd be cringing at the idea of my plane clothes touching the bed, but I don't have it in me.

Jess brought up a bottle of champagne and a bottle of white she slipped in the mini fridge. For being out in the middle of nowhere, this place is kind of cute. Cozy. Unique.

Seth sits next to me, looking at the weather on his phone. From here, all I see is a big blue blob on the radar that doesn't seem to dissipate, no matter how long Seth watches it.

"Damn. Not sure when this will let up," he says, quiet and almost to himself.

He takes up much more of this bed than I thought he would, but there's a thin gap of white between us.

"Food? Shower? What do you need?"

The way he asks me the question scratches my brain in the best way. It's like I can let go of a little bit of the tension taking residence in every muscle fiber. He's the one who braved the roads yet here he is, asking me what I need.

When my stomach rumbles, Seth doesn't miss a beat. "Food. Let's do it." He stands and grabs the room key. Our room is big enough, but he consumes more space than I expected—not in a negative way. His shoulders are wide, pushing tight against the fabric of his undershirt. I'm a fucking fashion icon with my Chanel slacks and matching vest, red bottom heels, and a men's athleisure top.

My phone buzzes—a reminder about my dinner reservation for tonight. I reply, letting them know I won't make it, and then it starts to hit me. My birthday plans? Completely derailed. The thing I've been looking forward to for so long has spun out of my control.

We make our way down the long hallway, peering out of the few windows scattered along the way. Night is in full force, the lightness of the snow trying to show through. A patterned runner grabs my attention beneath my feet—bold colors are the perfect vibe for the dark walls and wood. This is the kind of place I'm hoping to find when looking for a spot to stay–charming, unique, and afraid of beige.

Seth takes the lead in the kitchen, warming up the soup on the stove and easily moving around to find bowls and spoons. Typically, this would be me—leading the charge, making the decisions, and executing a plan. Instead, I lean on the counter, watching Seth move about the kitchen.

I swear, there's this permanent smirk that lives on his lips—one side playfully pulled up. His shoulders are broad, his muscles flex while he works, and he's light on his feet. When he puts his hand through his hair, pulling at the side of his neck, tilting his head as he stretches, it feels like there's sandpaper in my mouth.

I need another drink.

As I'm trying to swallow past the grit in my throat, Seth turns around and announces, "I've got the soup. You grab the bread?"

I nod, grab the plate of fresh bread—it's still warm from the oven—and the butter dish, following Seth into the dining room. Turning the corner, I almost stop when it comes into view. Candles are lit throughout the room, almost making it feel like it's glowing. The flames sparkle and reflect from a bay window, snow piling up on the other side.

The lights flicker as I sit in front of the bowl, steam rolling off the top.

"Candles are for more than the vibes, I'm guessing," Seth says, pulling his chair closer to the table. His forearms rest on the table and I have to remind myself not to stare.

It's clear: I need to get laid. It's been so long that I'm drooling over this poor man without him even knowing it. My insides clench as I think about the new vibrator waiting for me at home—a birthday treat to myself. Another part of my plan that will have to wait.

"So, what were your plans tonight?" Seth interrupts my thoughts.

Too quick, I defend, "What do you mean? What plans?" I grab a piece of the bread and try to hide the flush reaching my cheeks.

He turns, giving me a side eye and says, "Your birthday?"

Ah, he's just being a normal human, picking up standard cues. Clearly, I need to get a grip.

I put my spoon in the soup, cheddar cheese and bacon on the top, and some sort of potato situation underneath. Stirring, I watch the cheese melt and say, "Tonight was dinner at one of my favorite spots. I'll reschedule. Tomorrow, I had a whole spa day planned. It's been booked for six months because that's how long it takes to get an appointment."

"Fuck. I'm sorry you're missing it." He leans a little closer, and the way the candles show in his eyes is really fucking unfair. He has no business looking this good when we've been traveling all day. His fingers reach for the spoon and it's like I've never seen something hold a utensil before.

I make a mental note to download every single dating app when I'm back in the city because this is torture.

"Me too." I blow on the spoon, the steam still visible. I look for a wedding ring on Seth's hand but come up empty. "What about you? Anyone missing you at home?" I taste the soup, acting like I'm not fishing for information.

Shaking his head he says, "No. Just me. And off work until Willow gets back from Italy."

"Just what you wanted, spending your days off in Ridgeview, North Carolina?"

"In the middle of a rogue snow storm? Yes. You've nailed it." He laughs and something knots low in my belly.

I spread butter on the fresh bread, dip it in the soup, then take a bite. It's potato soup, but like a loaded baked potato—it's rich, thick, and heavenly. I feel like this is going to make the cold leave my bones. Sinking into the chair, I take another bite of bread doused in soup.

Anxiety from today—both air and land—nip at me, uncertainty and lack of control close enough to help give it the momentum it needs to take me under. I keep eating while Seth looks up at me every so often, that freaking smirk on his face, and I'm thankful.

Because this could be so much worse.

Six

Seth

I HAD TO GET away from Claire. So when the opportunity presented itself to clean up after dinner, I took it. Claire's currently in the room, taking a shower, and I'm washing the dishes. I try to focus on the suds, the smell of the soap, instead of where my mind really wants to go.

She kept pushing that thick bottom lip of hers through her teeth like a nervous habit. It was nothing but the two of us and her showing off that fucking perfect lip. All I wanted to do was taste it. Taste her.

The same way I wanted to pull her into my lap and tell her everything was fine while we were driving—not that it was even possible. My brain wrestled with the strong pull, almost like a string connecting us when I grabbed her hand on the plane. She had this energy about her, like she needed soothing. She needed someone to care.

I've always been able to tap into what people need. It's a blessing and a curse, depending on the day. A skill I've been able to tailor and use to my advantage across people and places. Call out what isn't quite right. Like when we were on the road and any focus I could spare was spent on everyone else—I was being a defensive driver.

Now, I'm stuck in some random place for who knows how long, with someone as gorgeous as Claire. I don't want to tell her, but the weather doesn't look like it's going to let up tomorrow. At least, not early enough for us to make the drive. I've got some contacts at a few large airports and when I told them about the emergency landing, they told me to expect flights to stay grounded tomorrow.

And it's her birthday. Fuck. I didn't know a ton about Claire prior to us spending the day together, besides the fact that people don't want to fuck with her. She knows her shit and doesn't get pushed around—another turn on. It seems like she prefers to be in control—a.k.a., this situation is her nightmare.

Standing outside the door to our room, I take a deep breath, letting my lungs stretch as much as possible while my heart rate slows. *I can do this.*

I knock on the door, letting Claire know I'm back before slowly opening it. The room smells like lavender and peppermint—has to be something from the shower—and the door to the bathroom is cracked open, light and steam filtering into the bedroom from the other side.

Opening my suitcase, I grab a pair of shorts to sleep in and wait for Claire to be done in the bathroom. Sitting on the edge of the bed, I think about how I'm going to be sharing a bed with someone for the first time in who knows how long. I can't even remember the last time I went on a date.

Pathetic. Or maybe just how I like it. Who fucking knows at this point.

My shoulders ache from the drive. I try to roll them out, loosen them up, and stretch my neck side to side. I'm pulling my neck, deepening the stretch, when the door to the bathroom swings open, steam escaping.

And then I'm a statue, unable to move or look away. Because there stands Claire in this black lacy piece of lingerie. It hits the top of her thigh and I know it barely covers her ass. Her full tits are snug in the top, her soft skin spilling slightly over.

She presses her lips together and looks around before clearing her throat. "I packed for Miami. This is all I have." Her eyes look down her body and now I'm cataloging her legs—thick, muscular, and skin I'm dreaming to touch.

I cross my legs, doing anything to hide the erection that's going to give me away any second now. It's been too long since I've been with anyone and seeing her like that? Knowing we're going to share a bed? What the fuck am I supposed to do?

"If you're uncomfortable, I can put the robe on over it." She crosses her arms over her chest, right where her nipples dare to show through the fabric.

"No, no. Don't. This is... fine." My words are flat and I swear I can see part of her shrink. "Wait, it's not fine. It's... you know..." *Seth, you fucking blubbering idiot, string together a sentence.* I look her up and down another time, giving my brain the time to compute words that will actually make sense. "You're gorgeous. If you want to pull the robe on, don't do it on my account, because that's not necessary."

Claire bites her bottom lip and I'd put money she's trying to hold back a smile. She walks over to what she's deemed her side of the bed, which coincidentally leaves my side open. Falling onto the top of the blankets, she sits, crossing her ankles at the end of the bed and smoothing out the fabric to cover as much of her as possible. Peeking at her, I can see a sliver of her ass peeking through the transparent fabric, the lace delicate and beautiful.

Her empty champagne flute catches my eye sitting empty on her bedside table. "Birthday girl, you want more wine?" I stand and reach for the chilled bottle. Part of me is nervous to see her reaction to me calling her that.

She giggles and it cuts through the tension in my chest—playful and light compared to the knotted worries in my muscles. "I'd love some," her eyes are on me with pink painting her cheeks, either from the hot shower or being embarrassed at me calling her birthday girl.

Claire lifts the flute and I carefully pour the bubbly wine. I fill it up, a little more than what's probably acceptable, and the bubbles quickly rise to the top of the glass. Claire puts it to her lips, slurping the top so it doesn't overflow.

"Hey! Too much." I can hear the smile in her voice as I put the wine back in the chiller.

I pick up my clothes and walk into the bathroom, turning over my shoulder and remarking, "There's no such thing when it comes to champagne."

The words are a reflex. Something I used to say in what feels like a previous life. They catch both of us off guard, for probably *very* different ways.

Before I can say anything else that brings me too far down memory lane, I shut the bathroom door and turn on the shower.

SEVEN

Claire

The champagne tastes like nerves—sharp, fizzy, a little too dry. It dances over my tongue in a way that feels mocking, like it knows why I'm drinking it. I take another sip anyway, the chilled glass almost slippery in my fingers.

The shower's still running and I'm having a hard time not thinking about how Seth is in there. Naked. Water running over his muscles.

Claire. Quit it. Think about something else.

My hands run over the comforter, heavy and cozy, perfect for the cooler months. I lean back, checking in with my body, noting how comfortable it is. Thank god. I couldn't handle the travel day we had then having to sleep on something like a soft version of a rock.

The bed. Singular. One. Just one. Maybe if I wish hard enough, it will split in two. I stare at it, waiting for it to suddenly sprout a polite little sign reading, "Don't worry, he'll take the floor!" I'd be next level asshole if I asked him to sleep on the floor, considering he went through the same amount of stress. Plus, if I'm being honest, I don't think I want him to.

That's the problem.

I cross my legs and uncross them again, tugging at the hem of the lingerie that isn't warm in the slightest. This would be perfect for Miami, but tonight? Not so much. Even with the shifting and tugging, my skin is on display and I'm cursing my light packing. It was going to be a quick trip, only a few days—our stylists had everything waiting for me for the events so I didn't have to bring much of anything. Jokes on me as I wear practically nothing, nervously listening for signs that Seth's done with his shower.

A positive is how much I adore this lingerie. It's from my favorite designer and it's the perfect blend of a delicate and stunning lace pattern with matching silk panties underneath. My hands rub down my thighs, pressing into the tight muscles and relishing in how good I feel in this.

The water cuts off. My stomach flips even though it has no business doing so. *Chill out. Knock it off. Be professional. This is a man you have to sort of work with.*

I stare at the empty glass on the end table, willing it to magically fill again. I'm too afraid to get up and have to rapidly cover my ass if Seth comes out.

I can hear him toweling off. The low hum of his voice as he mutters something to himself. His laugh—quiet, surprised, like he remembered something funny. I want to ask what it was.

Which is ridiculous. We barely know each other. We've crossed paths and been in the same place while working, but we've never had a serious conversation.

The bathroom door creaks open, and I look up.

He steps out in nothing but a pair of low-slung black athletic shorts, his skin still damp and glistening. Water beads trail down the sculpted lines of his torso—shoulders broad, chest firm, abs so sharply defined they almost look carved. There's a tattoo just under his ribs on the left side, a glimpse of dark ink I can't quite see all of from here.

His hair is wet and messy, pushed back like he ran a hand through it, but a few strands fall forward over his forehead. He slings the towel around his neck and catches me staring. I look up, too slow to be subtle.

His eyes find mine—dark, unreadable—but there's something there, something quieter than his usual smirk. And I swear, for a split second, he looks just as unsure as I feel but almost as if he's loving this.

I try to swallow past the sudden desert that's taken up residence in my throat, but it's like my entire nervous system just declared a state of emergency. Did I forget how to drink? Breathe? Function as a basic human being? My tongue feels like it's made of cotton and betrayal, and all I can think is: Please do not choke on your own spit right now. That is not the vibe.

"What?" he teases as he catches me staring.

"It's kind of unfair." I playfully slap the bed next to me before crossing my arms, trying to cover as much of myself as I can.

He turns his body side to side, like he's trying to stretch, and I am still trying to figure out his tattoo.

"What's unfair?"

I sigh out a low breath, looking up at the ceiling, scolding myself for not thinking before I speak. Why the fuck did I start talking? I'm usually much better at this. "You, looking like this. All muscles and your salt-and-pepper hair. You're all hot and mysterious—"

"Wait, you think I'm hot?" Seth leans closer to me, cupping his ear. "Is that what I heard?"

And he fucking winks at me. He's such a tease. It's like we're both playing a game, even though no one shared the rules or how we determine a winner.

"Seriously, do you need to do like five hundred crunches before bed or something? Don't let me stop you from whatever it is you do to look like that," I joke while counting his abs.

He laughs and it catches me off guard. It's honest and authentic and makes me smile to match him.

"No crunches tonight. I just like the gym. I like running. It's been part of my routine for so long."

Ah, so he's a runner. Believe me when I say, I would rather get a root canal than have to run. I've tried it—searching for the runner high people brag about—but all I got were blisters, sore muscles, and a level of boredom that's hard to explain. It's just not for me.

"Also, I like that you're telling me *I'm* the one who's being unfair when you're wearing that." He gestures to me, and I'd be lying if I said it didn't feel fantastic for him to look at me the way he is—eyes wide, the green vibrant in the hazel, and smirk painted on his lips, pushing his cheeks up. "You're the one who isn't playing fair."

Fuck me. My hands fly to my mouth, happy when I realize it was just an internal thought and not something I actually said aloud. I know my cheeks have to be red with how hot I feel, and I sense the color deepen when Seth brings the bottle of wine over, pouring some into my flute.

"Okay, birthday girl. What's the plan for tonight?"

There it is again: birthday girl. *Swoon.*

Looking at the clock, I'm surprised it's only eight o'clock. Damn, it feels so much later. Full day, that's for sure.

"We've got wine. Snacks..." He looks over to the basket waiting for us on the small bistro table in our room. "Can watch a movie. There's games in the lounge. Or, we can go to bed early. Completely up to you."

My muscles are tired; I'm certain I could fall asleep right now but I don't want to. The idea of spending more time with Seth is too enticing. Also, wine and snacks are always a good choice.

"If you were home, wrapping up your day, what would you do?" he asks, breaking my thoughts.

Using my new vibrator is the honest answer, but not the one I give.

"Honestly? Wine and a movie isn't too far off." I shrug my shoulders.

Seth smiles and I'm glad I'm sitting down because I'm on the verge of melting. He grabs his champagne, a few snacks from the basket, and slips into the bed next to me.

He fluffs the pillows behind him, propping himself up, and shimmies his shoulders when he settles in. I look over and I can see his tattoo.

Three numbers, black and bold.

171.

EIGHT

IF YOU HAD ME place a bet on where I'd end up tonight, it wouldn't have been on being in bed with Claire, in random-ass North Carolina, watching a scary movie with champagne in hand. This feels like I'm existing in an alternate timeline.

Never would've pegged Claire for the horror movie type, but we're thirty minutes into Scream, which I've obviously seen before. When she suggested it, I simply smiled as she pulled out her laptop, getting ready to play it. It wasn't what I expected but I think that's kind of her thing—she's not what anyone assumes. There was this moment where she almost waited for me to push back or tell her to pick something else, and when I didn't, I swear I saw her smile.

We slowly sip our bubbly wine and I do my best to steal glimpses of her. Her bangs are tousled, the rest of her hair framing her face as her head sinks into the pillow behind her. Before the movie started, she climbed under the blankets—I followed suit, mostly not to make it weird. But now, we're doing this weird dance where we know we're only inches away but don't want to touch the other.

It does help that she's not taunting me in that fucking lacy piece of lingerie—how could I pay attention to anything if that was an option?

Ghostface makes an appearance and she jumps, jolting us in bed, the champagne almost spilling from my flute. She laughs and groans, "Even when I know it's coming." Her fresh face is bright and bare, cheeks plump and pressing into her eyes. "I watch this movie more than what's even acceptable. It's one of my favorites." She turns towards me, almost like she could lay across my chest.

What the fuck are you doing, Seth? *Dreaming, obviously.*

Forcing my brain to pivot from thinking of her hand on my chest, I ask, "How often do you watch this? For real."

She sighs and covers her eyes with her free hand. "At least once a month." Splitting her fingers, she looks at me through the gaps.

"Wait, you're telling me that you watch Scream twelve times a year?" I gesture to the TV, the masked man chasing someone on the screen.

"At least. And not just Scream—all of it. The entire franchise. I love it." Shrugging her shoulders, Claire sips from her glass.

I can't help but let out the laugh that's straining my chest. "I would've never guessed that. Ever. I thought maybe you'd be into, like, arthouse or high brow shit."

She presses her lips together and glances at me sideways, "You would've guessed wrong."

I love how she's pushing back, playing the game.

"Honestly, it's not something I did until I started therapy. This is one of my coping mechanisms for anxiety—watching things I've already seen. My therapist suggested it, and it's become almost a routine now."

I nod along, even though I already know this trick.

"Emotional regulation. My therapist gave me the same tip, a million years ago at this point." I surprise myself with how easy it was to share something from the archives. Personal. Deep.

I can feel Claire's eyes on me, all light and golden. She doesn't say anything but instead lifts her glass, like she wants me to cheers her.

"To therapy." Her voice lifts at the end, almost unsure of what I'm going to do.

My glass clinks with hers. "To therapy."

We both take a drink, eyes locked on each other, because no one needs bad luck.

Claire sets her glass on her side table and settles in, pulling the comforter up a little higher, a grin on her face. I'm thankful she didn't press me, wondering why I found myself at therapy. No part of me is embarrassed—it fucking saved me.

Almost ten years ago, I was in the worst season of my life—a deep, dark, depressive sludge I couldn't shake. It's not that I keep it a secret, but no one in the city, or my new version of life, even knows who I was before this. What I lost. How I changed.

I'd tell them if anyone asked but I typically keep to myself. Part of me almost spilled my guts to the gorgeous woman next to me, but that certainly isn't a birthday type of conversation. We've had enough curveballs and let downs today.

By the time I realize how long I've been thinking about this, there's chaos on the screen, and I notice her flexing her fingers, rolling her wrists, and rubbing up her forearm. Looks like she's trying to relax sore muscles.

A few minutes go by; this time she's switched hands, and I do something I know is just asking for trouble.

"Give me." I reach for her hand, still looking at the laptop, trying to act like this isn't a big deal.

Startled, Claire questions, "Huh? Give you what?"

"Your hand. They're sore, yeah?" I keep my words level even though my heart thumps in my chest.

"Probably from holding on for my literal life on the plane. And again in the car. I'm fine." She admits this in such a way, it seems she's trying to convince herself she doesn't want my help, even though she winces when she stretches her fingers back.

"So stubborn," I grunt, almost under my breath, before lightly grabbing one of her hands and pulling it closer to me.

Claire tries to interject but all she gets out is, "You really don't… ohhhh," before she falls back as I start massaging.

Using my thumbs, I knead into her palm, feeling the tightness of her muscles. She moans as my fingers press and lightly stretch her hands. Immediately, I have to think of anything else because I'm about to have a full-on erection while watching Scream.

I run my hands slowly along her forearm, working my fingers into the muscles just below her elbow. Her skin is soft—smooth and warm beneath my touch. I can feel her start to relax as I press a little deeper, careful not to rush. There's a quiet tension there at first, but it eases with each movement. My fingers move in steady circles, following the shape of her arm, the way her body responds guiding my pace. It's simple, focused—just the sensation of her skin under my hands as she sits next to me.

My hands drop, letting her know I'm ready for the other arm. She moves closer to me, pulling her arm over her chest without saying a word. A quiet alarm buzzes through me, even though I'm smiling.

Because it's absurd how much I want to take care of her.

NINE

Claire

HIS THUMB WAS STILL moving. Not that I was watching it. Or thinking about it. Or—okay, I was absolutely thinking about it.

He was supposed to be rubbing my hands because they were sore. That's it. Practical. Helpful. Platonic. Honestly, my whole body feels like it's been through it from the worst flight ever followed by a horrific drive to the inn.

But that was fifteen minutes ago. And now?

Now we're under the covers, watching Scream with the wind raging outside, blowing through the windows like it's desperately trying to find somewhere to crash for the night. And Seth is holding my hand—gently, deliberately—his thumb brushing slow, lazy circles into my palm like he has nowhere else to be and nothing else to do.

And I am panicking. Quietly. Internally. In black lacy lingerie. My skin tingles where he touches it. Every pass of his thumb makes it worse. Or better. I can't decide.

He hadn't said anything after he told me I was being stubborn—he was right. Seth sits in those black athletic shorts—bare-chested, of course—like we weren't one blanket and one questionable decision away from something I definitely wasn't prepared for.

I need to get control back.

Clearing my throat, I suggest, "Okay. We need rules."

He turned his head slightly, not letting go. "Rules?"

"Yes," I state, with more authority than I truly feel. "Ground rules for the bed-sharing situation. To prevent any... weirdness."

Seth's voice is playful and rakes over my skin. "Define weirdness."

I roll my eyes at the fact that he's going to make me say it. Force me to draw the line we're trying not to cross. "Anything you wouldn't do with a coworker," I suggest.

"Hate to break it to you, but I certainly wouldn't be in bed with a coworker. Especially without a shirt on, or them wearing anything lacy." He shrugs his shoulders, but still draws shapes with his fingers on my skin. His smirk is mischievous—he's enjoying this.

"You know what I mean" I do my best to keep my voice firm, confident. He makes it hard for me to think. To want the things I typically do. "No unnecessary touching."

His thumb does another slow sweep across my palm, like he is trying to distract me on purpose. "So this is off-limits?" he asks, not stopping.

"Definitely," I say, except it comes out about thirty percent certain. "You're not even rubbing anymore. You're just... holding."

He smiles. "But giving you a massage? That was necessary? Even though I wouldn't do that with a coworker?" The way he's trying to play this game to end in his favor is unnerving..and delicious.

I scoff and hold back a smile, "You're being impossible." I try to pull my hand back to me, to at least have that type of control, but he holds it.

"I think *you're* impossible. With your lace and that fucking lip you chew on." He grins, baiting me.

The fucking lip you chew on. A detail I didn't expect him to notice or ever share aloud. My brain short-circuits for half a second. I pull in a sharp breath and sit up a little straighter, as if somehow my posture could save me from the emotional chaos unraveling beneath the blanket.

The walls seem to close in around us, pushing us closer and closer.

"Fine," I huff. "What do you suggest?"

"For rules?" He drops my hand and rubs his chin, like he's in deep thought. He turns toward me, leaning on his side, his tongue grazes his bottom lip. Seth goes to speak but then stops himself.

"What?" I press, almost desperate to know what he was going to say.

Pushing his lips together, he moves them side to side, and his eyes almost trick me to think they're green instead of hazel.. It feels like he's pinning me in place with his gaze. Silence grows between us, almost like a snowball, rolling down a hill of fresh powder.

Laughing to himself, he tips his head back and his Adam's apple bobs. "I'm trying to decide what answer I give you."

"What do you mean?"

"Well, I could give you the safe answer. Or, I could give you the honest one." His voice drops dangerously low, and quiet enough that I know he's being serious.

Shivers crawl up my spine, one vertebrae at a time. The seconds stretch and his eyes stay on me. All I can think about is how I don't want to fray the rope between us—the tension pulled taut.

"Your pick, birthday girl." His voice is pointed and it's holding me in place.

I take a deep breath, pretend like I'm thinking it over, but it's all for show. The second he mentioned the two options, I knew there was only one worth knowing.

Holding back a smirk, trying not to show all my cards, I tease, "What fun is it to play it safe when you know the truth?" The words feel like velvet on my lips.

Seth's mouth pulls up into a devilish grin, one that sends heat to my center, desperate for him to be closer. "I propose the one bed rule." The words are matter of fact—am I supposed to know what he means? Thankfully, he quickly continues. "When we're stuck here," he muses, gesturing to the room around us, "no matter how long it lasts..." He pauses and it might actually kill me.

I'm hanging on to every syllable, every twitch of his lip, every breath.

"We fucking give in." His voice is low and like gravel as his hand reaches to tuck a strand of hair behind my ear. Then his thumb is on my jaw while his fingers hold the back of my head.

There's no air, nothing to breathe in to relieve the ache almost cracking the bones in my chest. When his eyes go from mine to my lips, I can't help but do the thing he called out—I push the bottom one through my teeth, meticulously slowly.

He leans closer, eliminating the space between us, his hand pulling me gently closer to him. We're a short sigh apart; one move from either of us will change the game, the one I feel like we've been playing since we got here.

"Do you want to give in, Claire? Follow the one bed rule?"

I nod in agreement before the second question is out of his mouth. It's not a want at this point—it's a need.

His lips are close to mine; if I took a deep breath, we'd be touching. But he stops before kissing me and murmurs, "Need to hear you say it, baby."

Baby? Fuck. I am on another planet at this point. Whatever this man says, it's going to be a yes. The pivot from my standard need for control to whatever he wants is jarring but, in a way, causes flames to lick at my skin.

I answer, "Yes."

Seth offers me another smirk, one that has goosebumps raising on my arm, and then his mouth is on mine.

Ten

WHEN SHE GIVES ME the green light, a mental checklist forms of all the places I want to kiss her. Touch. Taste. Her lips are full when my lips meet hers—she leans forward enough to put herself into it. I push her so she's laying on the bed, her tits spilling over the cups of her lingerie. I brace myself, arms on each side of her, as I pull my hips to hover over her under the blanket.

This is what it looks like to go for it. Don't be timid. Don't hold back.

Claire's hands reach for me, pushing through my hair and almost pulling at me. "Kiss me," she breathes.

My lips crash to hers and we taste like champagne. When my tongue sweeps over her bottom lip, she opens, giving me access. She moans into me and I want to remember that sound—the way it hits me in my chest, how it makes my dick twitch. I tug her bottom lip, biting it a little, exactly the way I wanted to since I watched her do it.

I move my mouth to her jaw, kissing quickly until I'm at the column of her neck, feeling her pulse quicken underneath my lips. Playing with her, I lick and kiss, feeling her wiggle beneath me.

Letting my tongue go further, I lick all the way down until I'm at her chest.

Sitting back a bit, I take her in: eyes closed and she almost pants as she licks her top lip. When she feels me stop, her eyes open and they're deliciously wild.

"What are you comfortable with? Anything off limits?" I question, my erection pressing against my shorts when I sit back.

She props herself up on her elbows. "I have an IUD. Haven't had a partner in longer than I'm willing to admit, so I've been tested and am safe."

"I've not been with anyone either. I'm good for you, baby."

Claire is a goddess when she pushes her bangs back with one hand, her cheeks already pink with excitement. Fuck, she looks so beautiful.

"If you don't like something, tell me and I'll stop. It's that simple."

"Simple." She laughs to herself and falls back into the pillow.

I'm caging her body with mine, my lips a breath away from her tits. "Simple. Like, you said to kiss you. So, that's what I'm going to do. Kiss you." I lick her skin and then pepper kisses right where the fabric meets her fullness. "Here. And everywhere else." I look up and catch her watching me.

Hooking a finger at the top of the cup, I pull, exposing more of her while her breathing picks up. She's still watching me, and my eyes lock on hers as I take her nipple into my mouth. First I'm slow and careful, tasting her, feeling her skin respond beneath me.

When I bite, she moans out a *yes* and then I'm alternating between light kisses, bites, and taunting her with my tongue.

Claire moves beneath me, her hips lifting when I'm touching her just right. My other hand dips into her top and rolls the other bud between my fingers.

"Harder," she pleads.

"Yes, baby." I use more pressure with my fingers, biting harder on the one I've been worshiping with my mouth. She lifts her head off the pillow before falling back, and I know she loves this. And I'm trying not to lose it thinking of her giving me direction.

Her moans are falling on top of each other and I know the feeling. Wanting to slow it down, not having this be our finish. I leave her tits in the lingerie and move down her body. Stopping right above where her panties are, I place a slow and soft kiss over the fabric.

I push the lace fabric from the hem, her legs and panties on display. Feeling her eyes on me, I tease, "I love that you like to look." My mouth is dangerously close to her center. "And when you give me direction." I blow lightly, her nerves receptive as her eyes almost roll back. "Claire, I'm going to eat this pussy. Is that okay?"

"Yes," she whines.

"Anything you like?" I ask as I rub her upper thigh, skin way too fucking soft.

A look crosses her face and she lays back, no longer looking at me. "Ummm, I... I don't know." This time, she's quiet, and I can barely hear her.

"Where'd you go, baby?"

She sighs long and slow. I refuse to break the silence so I sit, my mouth in front of her lace, and I know if I were to touch her, she'd be dripping. When time stretches, she covers her eyes and groans, "I don't know why but I can never finish like this. There's something wrong—"

"Shh," I interrupt, not wanting her to even finish that sentence. "Do you make yourself come when you're flying solo?" I prompt her.

"Well, yeah..." Her voice fades as she still stares at the ceiling.

I reach and rest my hands on her hips, squeezing, wanting her to look at me. When she does, I say, "Then I think we'll be just fine."

She sits up again, "We can just... You don't have to—"

I rest my hand on her belly and lightly push her back. "Claire, lay back. Try to enjoy this as much as I'm going to."

Claire listens to me but I can feel her muscles clench. My easygoing girl who told me what she wanted when I was fixated on her breasts, is nowhere to be found. I want her back.

My hands grip her thighs, rubbing up and down, before reaching for the top and pulling her panties. I take them off slow, taking in every inch of her golden skin. I fold them and set them on the corner of the bed before coming back to her.

Licking my lips, I see she's trying to press her legs together.

"Bend these knees for me," I instruct. Claire follows directions and my mouth is practically fucking watering at the thought of tasting her. She pulls her feet almost to her ass and I praise her, "Good girl. Just like that."

I hear her take a deep breath and see her chest rise and fall quickly, like she's nervous.

"Any time you want me to stop, tell me. No questions asked." I reinforce the boundary and lick my lips. "Now, spread those knees. I want to see you, baby."

She pauses before moving one leg, and then the other.

"Fuck," I groan, mostly to myself, as I take her in. A fucking work of art.

I position myself with one hand wrapped around the top of her thigh and my other free to touch. Slowly, I insert a finger, and just like I suspected: soaked. That's where I start. My tongue enters her, trying to lap up all that wetness.

"Seth, that—"

I keep going. Licking slow, languid strokes around her entrance, letting her settle in.

"Feels good."

I smile and kiss around her center, not quite getting to the place I want to just yet. I lick her bikini line, the skin smooth and perfect, and I slip in two fingers. I pump them in and out, intentional and slow, trying to touch all of her, finding her spots. When I hook one of the fingers and touch her slightly differently, she lets out a moan that tells me everything I need to know.

Finally, my lips find her clit and while my fingers fill her, I kiss it gently and with almost zero pressure. My hand goes faster as I kiss a bit harder, her hips moving up to my mouth—pressing. Pushing the limit, I add a third finger and she takes them like a queen. Her walls are tight around them and I change from kissing to licking.

My tongue moves around her clit before I flick it, again and again.

"Seth, fuuuuck."

"You like when I use my mouth on you?" I moan to make her feel comfortable. I want her to be able to say whatever she wants.

"Yes. Your mouth. Your fingers." She whimpers and bites down hard on her lip before picking her head up to watch me.

Fuck. Don't come in your shorts. That's what I'm thinking when Claire ups the stakes and puts her hands in my hair. Her fingers tug and my own moan escapes my lips.

Eleven

Claire

How did we get here? We went from trying not to touch to Seth going down on me. My fingers pull on his hair as he brings me closer to the edge. He flicks his tongue before pressing it flat against me—alternating the pressure and the pace.

Shivers run up my limbs and back down my spine and it feels like I can barely control my body. My hips lift and tilt, my back arches, and my hands can't do anything but touch him. Seth feeds on me, and all these cues, and doesn't stop.

Even when he's stealing looks at me—which is ironic, because I'm doing the same to him—he doesn't quit. His eyes are fierce, a perfect match for the sly grin that keeps his lips dragging up. The man is smiling literally *into* me and this whole thing is spontaneous and ridiculously hot.

He turns his head and bites the inside of my thigh. I'm sure it's going to leave a mark and I sort of love it.

"Fuck!" The whine slips out of my mouth and a hand flies up to cover it.

"Don't cover that mouth. Let me hear you, baby." Seth coaxes me, cheers me on.

I glance at him and he's looking at me like a man obsessed, making me feel worthy of this attention. Fuck, I don't ever want him to look at me any other way.

The hand not filling me finds my thigh and he digs into it, grabbing, like he needs all of it. I put both my hands back in his hair and can't believe how good it feels. My nerves are fried but I chase my orgasm, like it's the only thing that will soothe the burns.

I can't help but whine and whimper as my climax is within reach and I pull Seth's hair like it will help me get over the finish line. He clues in and moans into me, the vibration pushing the tip of the wave over, and the world falls away.

It's like I'm flying—stars passing me by—and Seth keeps it up. My back arches off the bed and I'm holding onto his hair like it's a lifeline, keeping his mouth on me. The shocks keep coming, rocking me from the inside out, cracking me open and sending me falling into the abyss.

My chest rises and falls as I fight for oxygen and then Seth's hovering over me. He's kissing my neck, soft and slow, as his erection pushes into me. I'm so sensitive that I flinch when he touches me—but I can't get enough of it.

His smile is bright and a little bit 'I told you so,' and as I come back to the world around us, I know it's my turn to take control. For a second, doubt tries to push to the front of my mind, but I tell it to get lost—now's not the time.

Lightly, I push his shoulder until he takes the hint and lays on his back. The lingerie is too much for my skin so I pull the hem up and over, tossing it. Bare for him, I catalog his expression—one seemingly of awe. It makes me feel like I can do anything.

"Fuck, Claire." He groans while reaching his hand into his shorts, like he's going to stroke himself.

I don't think so.

Instead, I'm standing at the foot of the bed, and I reach up, pulling on the elastic band of his shorts. Once I pull them down and throw them on the floor, I catch my first glimpse of him. His cock stands at full attention, thick and veiny.

The just-fed need roars again and I'm hungry for him. I put one knee on the bed, in between his legs, and slowly crawl up on the bed. He watches me like it's his job; when I'm in front of him, I take another look at his length and the shiny bead of precum on the head.

Slowly, I situate myself on all fours, leaning on one hand and using the other to grab hold of him. The pressure is light, delicate, like I'm holding something that could break. His dick is heavy in my hand as I give it a squeeze and he licks his lips while watching me.

We don't break eye contact as I wrap my fingers around him and tip my mouth to that drop of wetness. Sticking out my tongue, I slowly lap it up before placing a kiss where it used to be. His muscles clench and I love that I can make him react like this.

My hand covers him at his base, my pinky close to his balls, and I take the tip of my tongue, pressing just enough for him to feel it, from the tip, down to my fingers, and back up again.

"Fuck," he growls and tips his head back, closing his eyes.

I do it again, top to bottom, squeezing my hand when my tongue is close. Next, I flatten my tongue a bit and taste more of him in the same pattern. Letting go, I brace myself on his thighs, kissing the head of his dick with a closed mouth. I plant a few kisses and then I catch his eyes, needing to know if he's watching me.

He is.

Just like I wanted him to.

I open my lips and take him in my mouth, as much as I can fit. His hands cover mine, still holding onto his thighs, and I try to take more of him the second time. And a third. Then I'm licking the veins, bulging, and making myself wet all over again.

This time, I'm going to push the limit as I put him in my mouth and try to get aggressive with how much of it I can cover. When I go too far, a gag comes from me and he whimpers.

Seth sits up and grabs my face, pulling our lips together. Crashing. Tasting. He's frantic and the way he devours me sends a shock to my core. It's like I'm air and he hasn't had a full breath ever, until right now, and I'm fucking eating it up.

But I'm still not satisfied. I want him. More of him.

I straddle him, my knees on each side of his hips, and he holds my ass, letting me take the lead. He seems to know I need it. He smacks my ass with one hand, playfully, and I let my entrance rub against his dick.

"Are you sure about this?" he asks, sitting up and taking one of my nipples in his mouth, his hands at my back.

"Yes." The word from my mouth doesn't sound like me.

He lays back and uses his hands to lift me over him. His cock nudges my entrance and I have no idea how much of him I'll be able to take. Inch by inch, he fills me.

"You're so tight. Still wet for me." His arms flex as he controls me on top of him and I don't know if I've ever been with someone this strong.

He's as gentle as he can be; it stings, but in a way that might kill me if we don't keep going. I move my hips, needing more, and can feel my walls stretch for him.

I breathe through it, deep and slow, my body tingling from the pressure. And then I'm taking all of him and he just stops, waiting for me to make the next call.

Slowly, I ride him, moving my hips forward, still stretching with his length. Seth's hands find my ass and he digs his fingers into my cheeks—hard enough to leave a mark. I throw my head back, finding my rhythm, my hands pushing into his chest.

He takes a thumb and puts it in front of my clit. When I rock forward, it hits me just right and I can't believe how close I am to coming again. My breathing is shallow, quick, and I can't help but chew my lip. I lift my chest, my hands finding my hair and pulling it, as Seth grips my hips with his other hand. I'm obsessed with the way his fingers dig into me, keeping the rhythm and pushing us closer together.

Seth pants, "I'm close. I'm—" His eyes are on me and I'm back to putting my hands on him, feeling his muscles flex underneath my fingers.

The slight lean forward, plus his thumb with the pressure, is all it takes for me to come again. This time it's slow and it drags me with it. My arms shake as I hold myself up, trying to keep my screams to myself, because we're not in someone's apartment—we're at a fucking inn.

Seth speeds up, causing my orgasm to hit me like a tidal wave, and then he's whimpering right alongside me. I feel him contract and flex deeper into me, the veins showing themselves on his neck as both of his hands find my ass.

He sits up, riding out his own shocks as I continue to push into him, needing more. Wanting everything he has to give. When the shivers leave my skin and I'm brought back to the two of us in this bed, I can't help but fall into him.

His hand wraps around me. "I like my rule," Seth whispers while rubbing my skin. I'm too spent to do anything.

Or even tell him he's right.

TWELVE

Seth

THE POWER WENT OUT an hour ago. I peek at my phone, seeing the time: 1:30 AM. I've been dozing on and off, as Claire moves around this bed like we've done it a hundred times. I got up when the power went out to get the extra comforter in the closet. Claire's back in her lingerie but she might as well be naked—it's definitely not keeping her warm. At first, she acted like she wasn't going to get close to me, but it took only a few minutes of her on her own, rolled away from me, for the cold to get her. Now, she's rolled into me, holding onto the arm that rests in the middle of the bed.

Looking over, I see her eyes flutter with sleep, maybe dreams, and can tell from here that her nose is red. It's fucking cold in here. I know Jess mentioned there was a generator, but maybe it didn't kick on? No way I'm going to go traipsing around, trying to find her; for now, we'll just stay warm until morning.

While I have a minute, I look at the weather app on my phone, making sure to turn down the brightness and keep as much of it away from Claire as possible. Don't want to wake her up.

How the fuck can it keep snowing like this? I watch the radar and it's this massive blob of blue that just keeps rotating but never really moving anywhere. It looks like white-out conditions are expected for tomorrow, and maybe even the next day. Pulling up the airports around us, I find all flights are still grounded. Nothing going in or out tomorrow.

Just when I think we could try and make the drive, slow and steady, there's a news article urging people to stay off the roads. North Carolina is not equipped to deal with ice or large amounts of snow like this. For fuck's sake, it's a good thing this place has a generator—one that I hope will at least work in the morning.

Part of me only suggested the whole one bed rule when I thought we'd end up making our way home in twenty-four hours. But, that would be too convenient, wouldn't it? Now, I'm going to be doing the "hang-of-shame" while we try to wait out a random ass storm in October? This would happen to me.

And it's not that I don't want to spend more time with Claire—because I do—but I'm kind of thinking about how we were with each other. Felt very much like a one time thing, for this bizarre circumstance only, and we'd go back to regularly scheduled programming and the city in the morning.

Taking her in, her lips still swollen and pink, there's this small crack in my chest, one that I'd barely feel if I was in my regular routine. Normally, I'd let myself feel it for a few seconds, take a deep breath, and move on. I've not had the space, time, or even want to feel much of anything like this.

That's what a massive loss will do to you.

It's been over ten years but still shapes so much of who I am, even when I think it doesn't.

Now, I'm thinking about how easy this was with Claire. How I didn't have to say much of anything to get her to jump in, head first. Maybe she felt the same way I was? Or maybe she was bored and didn't want to think about going to bed at 8 PM on her birthday.

All I know is that I haven't been with someone, this way, in a long time. Not even the sex— that was also something fucking wildly good and surprising—but the sleeping over, sharing a bed. I know this isn't what I picked, and it's just luck of the draw, but why can I see us doing this at my place?

Snap out of it, Seth. You'd never be spending the night with Claire if it wasn't for an emergency plane landing and a rogue blizzard in the fall in a place that doesn't really get snow. It's not like she chose to be here, or vice versa.

And as I'm doubting what this is, trying to get out of my own head, Claire stirs next to me. I try to settle in and act like I'm not wide awake.

Claire's arm unwraps from mine and fumbles to my chest. Slowly, it drifts from my chest to my shorts. She's rubbing me, the fabric separating her hands from my dick, and she moans in her sleep. Then her hand goes from the outside to slipping in, her fingers grazing me.

It doesn't take long for me to be hard and my eyes to find hers. She's awake, grinning at me, the sleep still in her eyes but still daring and like she's on a mission. One that I will happily help her complete.

First, she kisses my neck, her lips full and like velvet. Then she whispers, "Take your shorts off."

She says it like a dare, like she wants me to push back. There's no fucking way.

Once my shorts are off, my cock is hard and she's looking at it, and then back to me. She straddles me, her silky panties bumping into the head, and I can feel the warmth of her through the fabric. It's only a few seconds before she's moving down my body, settling in between my legs.

She's on her belly, holding her chest up, with one hand wrapping around me, one finger at a time. Claire strokes me, intentionally slow, I can feel it in the way she looks at me, like she's waiting for my reaction.

So, I give her what she's asking for.

"You've never looked better than you do right now," I praise, watching as she examines her hands, moving up and down my length. Claire flips her hair, it falling onto one side, giving me full access to what she's about to do next.

Carefully, she licks her lips, settles her hands at the base of my dick and then swirls her tongue on the head.

I let out a laugh, loving the way she pushes me. "I take it back. This is better." My abs flex when she strokes and licks, setting her own pace. If I know something about Claire, it's that she's known for doing things the way she thinks they should be done. She loves calling the shots and thrives with a decision.

My hands reach for her hair and she freezes. "No touching." She takes control, smirking up at me. Another thing I know about

Claire—her way is the best way, probably the right way, and who am I to argue?

"You can watch, though," she offers as her lips hover in front of the bulging head. I'm desperate for her to suck on it, put it in her mouth, move her fingers on me—I'll take anything.

I put my hands behind my head, clasping them and bending my elbows, doing exactly what I'm told.

Thirteen

Claire

I can't help that I'm bossy. But you know what? I don't think Seth minds; at the very least, he doesn't mind me waking up to give him a blow job in the middle of the night. The lights are off and the room is freezing—the power must've gone out.

My eyes have adjusted to the darkness, and I peek at the dips of Seth's core as he flexes and flinches while I surprise him with a light nibble. Giving head has never been my favorite, but there's something about this man that makes me want to take him, all the ways he'll let me. I think it's the way he reacts, honest and true, and it's like next level attractive.

Right now, I'm teasing him. Barely applying pressure with my hands or my mouth, just enough that he can feel it and want more. I know he's itching to touch me, his hands moving from behind his head a few times, but he puts them back behind his head.

"Good boy," I sweetly say with the head of his dick in my mouth.

"You're fucking unreal." He laughs in a way that I know he's going to make me pay for it later. Gladly willing to let him do that. The flames lick my core, thinking about him touching me.

I open my mouth and let my lips get as close to my fingers, still gripping his base, before I gag. He moans and I do it again. I'll do anything to get him to respond to me like this. Driving back down, I keep trying to take him, as much of it as possible. The head hits the back of my throat and I hold it, fighting the reflex before slowly pulling him out and slurping while I do it.

I know he wants to grab my head, fuck my mouth, and me making him keep his hands to himself is more fun for me. He sucks in an unsteady breath, short and ragged, as I keep taking him in and out of my mouth.

Taking a risk, I turn my head and move my hand up, so it's in the middle of his dick, and I lick where my fingers were just squeezing. And then I take one of his balls and put it in my mouth, moaning, so he can feel the vibrations.

He jerks in surprise but then lets out a slow and growling, "Fuckkkkk." One that gives me the answer I need, and I give attention to the other one. "That's so good. Your hands. Your mouth. I'm going to make this embarrassingly short." The last word squeaks out and his shoulders lift off the bed.

Back to this cock, I let my tongue move up and down as I stroke him in tandem. Then I take him in my mouth and breathe through my nose, letting me take as much of him as I can while trying not to gag. It's messy, and I wipe the back of my hand on my thigh, and the way he looks at me is something that's hard to shake.

It makes me want to keep going. Never stop. Watch this man come undone at the mercy of my touch. It's doing something special to my confidence, something people would pay for. Maybe they just need to suck the dick of a man who makes them feel like they can do anything?

Quicker, I'm sucking on him, and I let one arm hook around his leg, my fingers digging the inside of his thigh. A little pain and a little pleasure... one of my favorite equations.

His breath is quick, shallow, and inconsistent. "I'm close. Where do you—"

I pull away long enough to say, "I want it in my mouth."

And it's only a few more seconds until I feel his release building beneath my fingers. Seth gives me a final warning before I feel it spurt into my mouth, coating my throat. He shakes and jolts as he comes and I moan into his dick because it's hot. It's making me all needy and wet.

I'm about to swallow when he growls, "Wait. Show me."

This is a new one, I think as I gather his salty release on my tongue and open my mouth.

"You're fucking unlike anyone I've ever met," he says and I swallow him, feeling it slip down my throat.

I feel empowered, like Seth is someone who can match me—giving me what I need but letting me be the leader when I crave it.

Laying next to him, I watch his chest rise and fall as he comes down from his climax. It feels like something I do all the time. I curl into him, not trying to fight it.

"I'm serious," he grumbles, putting a finger under my chin and kissing my lips—the same ones that had his release on them just a few seconds ago. Hot. Again.

"I know." I smile at him, soaking in the praise.

FOURTEEN

Seth

THERE'S FROST ON THE inside of the windows—the generator kicked on but it's still freezing in here. It's almost 7:30 AM and the sun is still trying to break through the clouds as it rises for the day. I peel myself from Claire, quick to pull the blankets up and around her.

Grabbing a long-sleeved shirt from my bag, I throw it on and make sure to unlock the door so I don't need to bother with a room key. Slowly, the door shuts behind me and I'm careful not to make a ton of noise.

I'm in my socks as I pad down the stairs, waiting for the clues that anyone else is here or around this early. There's nothing.

I'm standing in front of the espresso machine, which is much nicer than I thought it'd be. Filling it with espresso beans, it seems like it will automatically grind and let me pour a shot in just a few minutes. I'm not a fiend like Claire, but I've been around my fair share of coffee machines. Sometimes in my line of work, you have to stay up for days at a time, and caffeine is the only way around.

While the espresso works, I go to the kitchen, finding a container of skim milk—which is how I know Claire takes her coffee. Well, her cappuccinos, to be exact. The espresso machine has a milk frother and I use it to steam the milk and create the foam.

It's weird how easy it was to wake up and immediately want to do something for Claire. Part of me is wildly aware that her birthday plans were ruined, so if there's something I can do to make it not suck so bad, why not?

Plus, Abigail was always big into birthdays. She loved to bake, show up with breakfast on a tray, and grin like she hadn't been in the kitchen for hours already. I loved her like that: flour on her nose, and a look on her face that was just itching to see if you liked whatever she put together. Everyone always did—she was an amazing cook.

Even now, she makes me better. Even after all this time.

The milk is ready and I pour it over the espresso shot. The foam is thick and fluffy, reminding me of the clouds during the summer. I go to work on another shot of espresso—this time, I fill a kettle with water, boiling it for my americano.

The smell of the coffee, the richness of the beans, wafts through the space. I rest my hands on the outside of the kettle and let it warm my fingers. I get lost in the bubbling of the water, waiting for it to boil, when someone walks in.

A hand flies over Jess' mouth, muffling her shriek. "Oh my goose neck. You scared me." She tries to whisper but it's damn near a speaking volume. Her hand rests on her chest, like she's trying to catch her breath.

"Sorry. I didn't mean to. Just making some coffee."

"No need to apologize, I'm the one who's on edge." Her hands rub her arms over her long-sleeved shirt, like she's trying to trap the warmth. "Obviously," she looks around the room, "the generator has been hit or miss. And, the roads are so horrible that our chef won't be able to make it in." She peeks around me to look into the kitchen. "I've got pastries and some fresh fruit for you, but if you want to use anything in the kitchen, you're more than welcome."

"We should keep checking on the fridge and freezer. Like, make sure the generator is working so we're not about to eat spoiled food," I suggest.

Her face is soft before her brow furrows, the way your mom does when you offer something you know she won't take. "*We* won't be doing anything. You're the guests. I'll keep an eye out on things like that."

Pouring the hot water into my espresso, I nod. "Sure. But if you do need anything, please don't be afraid to ask."

Jess hands me a small tray for the two coffee mugs, and I carefully set them on there, before taking it with both hands. Carefully, I walk it up the stairs, looking ahead and not at the liquid in the mugs—a trick I've heard helps to reduce spilling.

When I reach the door, I carefully grab the handle, doing my best to balance the mugs, and push it open. Immediately, I set the tray down on the bistro table, not wanting to press my luck any further. In the bed, Claire stretches as her eyes pop open. She sits up, almost in a panic when she realizes I'm not in bed with her, but she quickly relaxes once she finds me.

"What are you doing?" she asks, wiping her eyes.

"Coffee?" I offer her the cappuccino and watch as her lips pull up in a lazy smile. "Cappuccino. Skim milk," I say with a sweetness that I know is unnecessary. Part of me simply wants to see her face when I nail her coffee order.

She fluffs the pillows behind her, resting her back so she can sit up, and reaches for the cup like it's a lifeline. I hand it over, trying not to laugh at her caffeine dependency, and put my own mug on my bedside table.

"You know my coffee order," she states, taking a sip.

"Well, I think I heard someone get yelled at over it while attending a meeting you were also at."

Her head is on a swivel, looking at me. "I never yelled at anyone over coffee."

"No. Not like that. More like they didn't want to disappoint you or rub you the wrong way, so they were doing the pre-yelling, because someone else messed it up." I clink my mug to hers and take a sip of the americano—smooth, strong, and perfectly warm.

Tilting her head, her voice is less urgent this time. "Oh, okay. That makes sense." She takes another drink from the mug, and I can't help but admire her lips.

This is the part of Claire I've always found interesting. I've really never heard her yell at anyone, not even raise her voice, but people act like she's someone they certainly don't want to cross. It's like, you just get it. You accept that she's in charge, she knows what's going on, and she will take no shit. I like that she can hold her own.

It's the quiet ones you have to watch out for.

Fifteen

Claire

NOT ONLY DOES HE deliver earth-shattering orgasms, but he also brings coffee. How is this man single? It makes no sense to me.

The heat has tried to kick on since we've been back in bed, but it only runs for a minute before turning off—likely not having enough power to really make a difference. I'm cursing the lacy lingerie I packed because this isn't the time for it. My hands hold the mug like it's precious, not only for the jolt of caffeine but also for keeping my fingers from turning into icicles.

"Come on, I know you want to get closer," Seth teases, an arm open.

I slide over, careful with my mug, and sink into him, warmth radiating from his body.

The memories from last night hit me and bring a flush to my cheeks. Hey, a little morning embarrassment may be perfect when you're trying to get warm. I'm quiet as I mentally run through it again.

Why am I embarrassed? I shouldn't be. We're two consenting adults... who feasted on each other like there was nothing else to eat. I fucking woke this man up in the middle of the night because I couldn't stop thinking about him in my mouth. This feeling of not being able to get enough is new for me. Typically, I can hook up with someone and it's sometimes so mediocre I'm thinking about something else *during* the act. Sort of thought that's how most of these things went. Until last night.

Plus, he started it.

And by the look of what's happening outside, and what I've read from the news outlet, the one bed rule might be in play for another day.

What a shame, I think, and immediately start laughing to myself. Surprised that my anxiety isn't skyrocketing, thinking about my plans being derailed another day. Luckily, I have nothing scheduled that can't be moved. Willow already texted me when she noticed my location was somewhere in North Carolina, not back in the city.

She asked me to send her photos of outside because she didn't believe it. The snow dances as it falls, pretty against the mountain and trees in the background. The sun is starting to show through, making the flakes look like glitter that's trickling from the sky.

I move, a little sore from last night's festivities, and start to giggle. It's like there's this secret between us and I wonder if one of us will break first. Will we talk about it? Or will we move around each other like he didn't come in my mouth and then ask me to show it to him?

"What's so funny?" Seth asks just as my stomach starts to growl. "Okay, food next." He closes his eyes and sits back against his pillows.

I do the same, the heaviness of the blankets making it hard to think of getting up, even for food. The way we can simply be together, the quiet swirling around us, is remarkable. I'm the type of person who reads menus before going to a restaurant, plans out where to park or be dropped off if I've never been somewhere before, or gets into a hole of reading reviews of a place before finally booking. I like to know what's coming next and be mentally prepared.

This is the opposite of that.

Well, I did immediately look at the weather and come to terms with the fact that we're not getting on a plane today, and I'm certainly not ready to get into a car with the roads like this. No. No way. I'm good. At least for now.

SETH IS IN THE kitchen, making us breakfast, when Jess finds me sitting at the table. She's holding something as she says, "I heard you say you were stuck from Florida. I found these in storage." She unfolds a crewneck sweatshirt with the inn's logo on the front. "I guessed on sizes, but if you're interested, they're yours."

I reach for the smaller size, the fabric plush and soft underneath my fingers—this is a good sweatshirt, especially when I'm wearing one of Seth's long sleeves and my dress pants.

"Thanks. You can charge them to the card we used at check in," I suggest while folding the two sweatshirts up and stacking them on the table.

Shaking her head, she presses, "No way. Seth is making my breakfast and this is less than an ideal stay. Don't you worry about it." Her shoulders shrug.

"Thank you. Honestly," I reply while not wanting to push the issue.

Seth rounds the corner carrying plates like he works in a restaurant, one in each hand and the other resting on his forearm.

"Omelettes," he announces, carefully putting a plate in front of me and reaching for the other to hand to Jess.

Part of me thought she'd sit down with us, but instead, she thanks him and leaves us to it. Seth slides into the chair across from me and says, "Kept it simple with some cheese and roasted potatoes that were in the fridge."

The omelette looks perfect; the cheese is melted and the smell of potatoes, salt, and pepper makes my mouth water. Damn, this man can cook.

"Were you a chef in your past life or...?" I jokingly ask, as I take a bite and relish in how great it tastes.

Smirking, he answers, "No. Just a firefighter. I was the go-to in the kitchen, so I picked up a thing or two."

There's this moment where something flashes in his eyes. It's hard to place, but it felt like there was more to the story and he cut it short. I mean, there's a reason he's not a fire fighter now, and I can't imagine some of the things he must've seen. Maybe it's hard to go back to that time in his life? I try not to dwell on it and instead practically inhale the omelette.

He watches me over his coffee, then grins. "So, you really are a rule follower, huh?"

I shrug, pretending to be very focused on my omelette, but I was sort of waiting for him to bring it up. "I mean, you made the rule, knowing damn well who I am."

He laughs over the coffee mug, "To be honest, part of me thought you'd tell me to get lost." His shoulders shrug.

I glance up. "Wow. So you're *that* guy. Makes the rules just to see if someone will break them."

He sips his coffee slowly. "Not typically. But I was very eager to see if you'd follow it." The words from his mouth roam over my body, itching me to get closer to him. The way his gaze pins me to this spot–he knows what he's doing.

Fuck it. I'm just here to follow the rules.

Sixteen

Seth

Claire and I are wearing matching The Fable Inn sweatshirts and trying to stay warm in front of the fireplace. The crewnecks are this dark green color, one of my favorites—nothing like getting a little souvenir from being stormed in.

The sounds of tiles hitting the board pull me back to our scrabble game.

"Wait. You can't play that," I argue, as the word BLOWJOB stares up at me. She added the 'JOB' to 'BLOW' which I played a few turns ago.

"So, you're telling me this isn't house rules?" She sits back, waiting for my response.

"House rules? We're at some random inn." I gesture to the room around us.

"Fine, inn rules. Even better. You can play any words you want. Slang, whatever, as long as the other person has heard of it."

I nod along and it's hard not to agree with her.

"I assume you've heard of a BLOWJOB. Yes?" Claire teases me, looking down at my shorts, and back up again.

She says it in a way that heats my blood, knowing she had my dick in her mouth only a few hours ago. It's hard not to get distracted when she looks at me like that.

"Yes. Heard of them. Big fan actually." I grab the notepad which we're using to keep score and wait for her to count her points. "Do you get credit for what you added or the whole word?"

"Whole word," she's quick to reply. "Obviously." There's the confident side of her I've always been enamored with. There's something incredible about a strong, confident woman like her.

I like her this way. All light and funny. No part of me could've ever seen this coming, playing a game of Scrabble where Claire just played an oral sex term, while wearing matching crewnecks. Even if I wanted to run, there's nowhere for me to go.

But I don't want to.

Besides run her upstairs to our room. Have her all to myself.

After a few more turns, it's clear that Inn Rules for Scrabble is the way to go. Normal words like COURT, CURTAIN, and DECK, easily mix with TITS and CUM.

The game is really close, score wise, and we're running out of tiles. I've got a perfect opportunity to use almost all of my tiles. And maybe get a little more of what I want. What I'm craving.

Placing the tiles, one at a time, I play the word SHOWER. It lands on a triple word score; that might be the game and Claire knows it.

"Damn. That's a good play," she muses, watching me count the points and add it to my score.

Leaning in close, my lips are barely an inch from hers, and I love that she doesn't flinch. Her eyes match mine and she pushes her lower lip through her teeth. "That could also be our next activity."

She surprises me by kissing me quickly. Her lips hover for just a blip as she says, "Only if you make me..." as she points down to CUM.

Fuck. She's good.

Claire stands, her tits almost eye level with me, and she hands me the bag, sliding the tiles from our game in—don't need Jess stumbling upon our saucy playing rules.

I reach for her hand, which she takes, and we walk back to the room.

When the door closes behind us, I lock the door. I hear the water turn on in the shower—Claire must be eager—and the thought of her has my dick twitching.

She walks out and pink starts to creep on her cheeks when she looks at me. Claire stands, crossing her feet, and clasping her hands in front of her. Almost like she's nervous.

We can't have that.

I stand in front of her, smiling, and say, "Arms up."

With zero hesitation, she listens to me, and I grab the hem of the sweatshirt and pull it up and over her head, before going back for my long sleeve she was wearing underneath.

Then she's standing there, nothing covering those perfect tits. For a second, she tries to cover herself up by crossing her arms, but my hand is reaching for them.

"Don't you dare," I demand. I pull her arm away and then put my mouth on her. I suck and lick at her pebbled skin. Trying to pay equal attention to each breast. Claire's hands wrap around my shoulders and she gives into me, pushing her chest out.

She moans and it goes straight to my dick, the steam coming from the bathroom and curling around us. Needing to be touching her, more of her, I take off my sweatshirt then make quick work of my pants. Claire follows suit until she's standing in front of me in only a pair of panties: red, lacy, barely there.

Claire turns and walks towards the bathroom, her ass on display for me. The thong wraps around her hips and is showing off all of her curves. When we stand in the bathroom, I can't help but take off my briefs.

She watches me, licking her lips as she stares down at my cock. Claire sucks in a breath as I step closer to her and murmur, "You need help with those?"

When she nods, I hook a finger at each of her hips, slowly dragging them down as I drop to my knees. I'm torturing myself with this pace but the nervous energy rolling off her is fucking worth it. I'm careful to only touch her with my fingers, down her legs, even though my mouth passed right in front of the place I couldn't stop thinking about.

She steps out of the lacy thong and I slowly stand up, making sure to only rub up her legs with my hands. When I'm standing, she wraps her arms around my neck, and pulls me into her for a kiss. My dick hits her stomach as she kisses me like I'm the air she's been trying to grab for days.

My hands go from her hips to her thick ass. I squeeze and grab her cheeks, round and firm, before giving one a playful slap.

"Harder," she pleads into the kiss.

I spank her, my hand stinging a bit this time, and she whines into me. "Good girl, telling me what you want."

The shower is a walk-in style with a small bench. It's surprising, like most of this place. Carefully, I walk her in, her back being hit with the warm water first. We don't break our kiss as the water hits us from two different shower heads—one of them detachable.

Immediately, the ideas are overflowing from my brain—all the things I want to do to her. All the ways I want to fuck her.

"You know the thing about good girls, right?" I ask.

She shakes her head.

I lick her lower lip, the one she chews when she's nervous, and put my hand above her, pressing into the tiles. "Good girls get to come first."

SEVENTEEN

Claire

I FEAR I'M ONE touch away from unraveling and nothing has even happened yet. Seth's words wash over me, tingling my skin. The way we've shared control is killing me in the best way. I love that we've gone from me waking him up in the middle of the night, to him suggesting shower sex through a game of Scrabble.

Seth's mouth finds my neck and he kisses and sucks. He's gentle and I want more.

"Don't hold back." I whine, pushing my hips into him.

In my ear, he whispers, "You want me to leave a mark?"

"Yes." The word is needy and fucking desperate—I'm surprised it came from me.

And then he bites the soft skin at the start of my shoulder. He sucks, making sure I get what I want, and I swear I could come from him touching me like this.

His tongue circles the spot and he bites again; this time a hand reaches up and pinches my nipple—his nails digging into the soft skin. I don't need to ask him for more because he already knows what I'm looking for.

Panting, I put my hands on the sides of his face and put a searing kiss to his mouth. Seth grabs the hair tie around my wrist, lightly pulling it off, and turning me to face the shower head.

His chin rests on my shoulder, lips almost touching my ear lobe while he turns in and says, "Tip your head back." I do what I'm told; to my surprise, his fingers pull my hair up and away from my face. Seth tugs the hair together, wrapping the hair tie to keep it secure, and then reaches his hands in front of my body.

His fingers push into my skin, starting right underneath my chest, until they rest on my thighs. Seth draws circles with his thumbs while he uses his lips on my neck. I feel his length pressing into my ass, and I can't help but push further into him.

When his hands move to the side of my hips and then my ass, I feel him lower behind me. A small wave of nerves hit me just as he says, "Put your hands on the wall. Bend over."

His voice is like a jolt to my system—he's firm but still gentle and I'm worried he could get me to do anything, which is not my normal attitude. I'm the person who loves to analyze, figure it out, determine what is the smartest decision. Meanwhile, Seth could tell me to try and do a backbend in this shower and the only thing I'd check is if there's enough room for such a thing.

My hands find the tile and I move my hips back. When it's not enough, his hands wrap the front of my thighs and he pulls me back even further. His lips kiss the back of my legs, soft and gentle, and it's the contrast of the position and the sweetness of his actions.

I'm on full display—each touch of his lips, fingers, making me needier by the minute. My brain waits for the doubt to creep in, crash in around the feelings of bliss and want. But with each kiss, touch, moan from his lips, it's nowhere to be found.

Seth's hands stay on me but I'm missing his mouth–the way he tastes me. I'm trying to look behind me, but it's not really possible. And then his tongue laps at my entrance. The sound that bubbles from my chest is full and desperate.

"Soaked. Just like I hoped," he groans between licks, twirling his tongue.

The flutters in my belly are quick and leave behind an ache. Seth teases me by taking his tongue and mouth away before bringing it back, touching me differently than before. His hands roam and I love how it makes me feel—he moans like he wants me.

He circles my entrance with his mouth before inserting a finger. And then another. He pumps slowly and it keeps pushing me closer to the break I need.

But then he's gone. Looking to my right, he's sitting on the bench, his dick hard. When he wraps his hand around himself, stroking, my mouth waters, thinking about having him last night.

"On my lap." He pats his thighs, spreading them further apart.

I'm standing in front of him when he suddenly tells me, "Turn around."

Soaking in the direction, I turn until my ass is back to him. Seth's hands find my hips and he slowly pulls me to him until he's just touching my entrance.

Oh. This position isn't what I expected.

I take a slow, deep breath and mentally prepare. The soreness from last night sparks for a few seconds but it's not enough to stop me from going through with what's next.

"Breathe through it, baby," Seth coaxes, and I close my eyes, slowly taking him inch by inch. He stretches me and the hurt from last night's events has me biting my lip and wanting to rub my clit. I want all of it.

"Up," Seth demands.

I stand up, him slipping out of me, my wetness making it easy.

"Back down," he says just as he's out of me.

The second time is easier, my muscles making room for what they can.

Without being told, I do the same thing a few more times, trying to keep the pace patient. Each time I sit back, taking in his cock, it's easier. Feels better. Instead of holding my breath, waiting for the discomfort, moans are slipping out of my mouth.

Seth grabs the detachable shower head which is right next to us. He plays with the settings until he finds one he's satisfied with.

He hands me the shower head. "Now, be a good girl and use that on your clit while I fuck you."

The words barely register in my brain until I'm holding the shower head with one hand, the other still bracing myself on his thigh. His hands grip me and he starts lifting me and putting me back down on his dick.

So *that's* what those muscles are for.

The stream from the shower head is just the right amount of pressure. I test it on the inside of my thigh as Seth continues to fuck me while I sit on his lap.

"Don't make me wait." He bites my shoulder. "You need to come first." He says it like it's non-negotiable. Another rule.

One I'm begging to follow.

Eighteen

Seth

CLAIRE DOES WHAT SHE'S told and moves the shower head in front of her. I look around her body to see her testing the pressure on her legs before letting it touch her clit.

"Ugh, fuck." She practically groans in approval as she uses one hand to hold the shower head and the other is bracing herself as I continue to move inside her.

We've found a rhythm, her leaning forward enough, and I can push inside her from here. Her moans vibrate through her chest, and I feel it from sitting behind her. It has my balls tightening at the thought of her letting go.

My body aches with the need to come. Feel her come around me. Hear those moans she makes when she's losing herself.

"Play with your tits," I instruct and the words are barely out of my lips before the hand bracing herself is rolling her pink nipples.

Without the bracing, she fully takes me; takes every inch of this cock that's getting too close to coming. I meant what I said: she comes first.

My hands grip her, lifting and pulling her back down, as she uses the shower head on herself. She's damn near panting when I say, "Look at you. This greedy cunt taking all of me."

"Yes," she whines, dragging the words. Her voice almost begging has me one step closer.

Don't fucking come before her.

Her breathing is shallow and then she's holding her breath but moving her hips on me, desperately searching for what she wants. I know her orgasm has to be close because her core flexes, her legs holding herself in just the right spot. I tip her hips forward, just a little, and speed up.

"Need you to come so you can bounce on this dick," I growl, my voice stronger than I intended.

But that's what does it. I feel her contracting around me, her head falling forward as I keep pushing into her. Her pussy grips me tight and that's what it takes for me to chase right after her.

Claire bounces on my cock; the feeling of her around me and the moans that fall out of her mouth send my own orgasm ripping through me. My hips push harder, needing her to take all of this, everything I'm spilling into her. Then I feel the shower head on my balls, Claire now rubbing her clit to finish out her climax.

The water is hot and strong—the pressure a fucking perfect match to the gorgeous woman on top of me. It's tunnel vision, the rest of the room, or shower, nowhere to be seen.

Her head falls back, resting on my shoulder, and the weight of her has my heart thumping in my chest so loudly I feel like she has to be able to hear. The shocks stop and our moans die down when Claire puts the shower head back where it belongs.

For a few seconds, we sit with my cock still buried in her. She tries to catch her breath and I give her a gentle kiss to her shoulder blade. I swear, she pushes back into it.

"Now stand up and let me see you." My voice is jagged and deep.

My girl loves to listen—she stands, slow, her legs trembling just enough for me to see. She tries to turn to face me and I lightly grab her hips, stopping her.

"Not yet," I say, my eyes glued to the inside of her thighs.

And that's when I see it, my cum leaking from inside her. It's like something cuts through the steam and the feeling sprints through my bloodstream—how much I want her. Again. And again.

Like she's not close enough.

"Now that's a beautiful sight." The words are mostly for myself, but obviously Claire hears.

Her voice is breathy as she turns her head over her shoulder to ask, "What is?"

"My cum dripping from you like this." I see her smile, her cheek giving her away.

I stand, spin her around, and then fuse my mouth to hers—needing a taste. She kisses me back, looping her arms around my neck. Claire bites my lip and hangs on to me, tighter as each second goes by. My hands roam from her hips to her low back and I pull her into me.

And then we stand there, surrounded by steam. Part of me feels so full and like I'm getting something I've needed for a long time. Good sex? Good company? Both? Fuck, who knows. And honestly, at this point, I don't care to dissect it.

I rub circles on her back and there's still this pull to her. Like I want to take care of her, even though she's damn well capable of doing that herself, and would have no problem telling you that. I kind of like seeing how I can make her break a little, see how far she'll let me go.

"Now, let's get you cleaned up," I say, while guiding her into the stream of water.

My hands reach for the brand new loofah and I put body wash—vanilla and peppermint—on it. The bubbles form fast, the lather like velvet between my fingers.

And just when I think she's going to tell me she can do it herself, or that I don't have to do that, she simply gives in, "Whatever you say, Seth."

NINETEEN
Claire

I DON'T KNOW WHERE I am but whatever I'm holding onto is like my own personal heater. Lifting my head up, I see Seth, looking at me, Scream playing in the background.

"You made it about fifteen minutes and slept through the rest of it," he teases me.

I try to look at the clock to check the time, but there's nothing. The room is quiet besides the sounds from my laptop—ominous early 2000s music from the soundtrack to be exact.

Like he can read my mind, Seth says, "No power. Generator went off. Jess came up and said someone will come and get it right by the time tonight rolls around. Good thing we charged your laptop, huh?"

Damn. I don't know what's more surprising: that I took a nap or I missed someone at the door.

When was the last time I took a nap? Couldn't tell you. Being manager for one of the biggest celebrities in the world doesn't lend itself to taking many breaks.

My body sinks into Seth, his arm around me, the smell of vanilla still on our skin. The grin that hits me is almost embarrassing, thinking of us in the shower. Him cleaning me up after practically becoming feral with seeing his release on my skin. And then the flip to taking care of me, even rubbing my shoulders, the knots still present from tumultuous travel days.

How is this man single?

My stomach growls and there's nothing to muffle the sound. Seth laughs as he offers me a plate. "Jess brought up peanut butter and jelly sandwiches... all from scratch. They make the freaking peanut butter." He shakes his head while I sit up and take the plate. "You're lucky I like you enough not to have eaten both of them."

You're lucky I like you.

The rush of his words wash over me, like his hands did earlier. My head feels like it floats while my skin touching him grounds me to the moment. And if that wasn't enough, his hand rests on the top of my thigh and squeezes.

"Yahtzee!" I yell, seeing the five dice match. Threes have been hot this game.

Shaking his head, Seth grabs the dice. "You might win this one."

We're downstairs in the lounge, playing games in front of the fire. There are a few candles lit and a battery powered lantern, making it easy enough to see. Seth won the first game we played and I'm about to take the second.

According to Jess, she wants to wait until we're almost ready for bed to run the generator. The weather hasn't let up and part of me wishes I had boots and warmer clothes so we could play in the snow. How often could you say you built a snowman before Halloween?

It's alarming how we've slipped into this couple façade. Like, his hand grabbing mine when we walk down the stairs, or the thigh squeezes, or the fucking way his eyes look when they land on me, more green than hazel today.

We sit fireside in matching crewneck sweatshirts, playing games and drinking hot toddies. Jess promised they were her specialty and she isn't wrong. I've had this cocktail before, but there's something different—I can't quite place it—and I know I'm right, because she's been teasing a secret ingredient.

All I know is they're delicious.

A grandfather clock in the room squawks and tells us it's 5 PM. Back home, it'd kill me to not know where my day went. My brain would be screaming at me to be productive— don't waste it. But I think orgasms and hot showers in an October storm, followed by a divine nap plus the end of my favorite scary movie is anything but wasting a day.

We tally our scores as Jess leaves a tray of fresh bread, fruit, pretzels and butter. I love how unbothered she is by this whole thing. She's so sweet and has been doing anything she can to make us more comfortable. It makes me want to come back to The Fable Inn but as an intentional destination.

The fire crackles and I know I beat Seth by the way he's tilting his head, glancing at me as I finish my score.

"We're tied. Have to do best of three." Seth claps his hands, rubbing them together. "But you won, so you get to ask me two questions. Anything you want."

The terms we set before we started rolling any dice was the winner got to ask the loser two questions. Seth's first win resulted in me sharing the celebrity I can't stand to see when I'm working (I hate that he was in Parks and Rec) and my favorite childhood cereal (Captain Crunch).

Now, it's my turn.

"Your tattoo. The numbers. What do they mean?" I ask as I take my first roll.

His face dulls for just a second, almost like something slipped. He takes a deep breath, sighing it out, and answers. "It was for my station. When I was a firefighter. Got them with a few of the guys."

"Do you still keep in touch?" I quickly burn my second question.

He pauses for just a second as I finish the last roll of my turn. Seth takes the dice and shakes them, before continuing, "We try. Hard when they're in Michigan and I'm in New York but we try to get together at least once a year."

"I love that," I say, thinking of Seth getting loud with a bunch of his friends. Before this getting stuck together situation, I could've never pictured it.

I'm the one who doesn't have many friends by choice. Especially with my job, it's hard to know peoples true intentions and I've been burned too many times to hand out chances like I used to. The thing it's taught me is how much I'm okay with being alone. Sometimes, you need to learn to sit and love yourself in silence before expecting anything else from anyone.

The fire crackles as Seth rolls the dice.

Maybe it's time to let someone fill that silence.

TWENTY

Seth

APPARENTLY, THE KITCHEN RUNS on its own generator. Jess let us know she'd kick on the other one in an hour and make sure it runs all night. The roads are covered with inches of snow but the layer of ice underneath is the real problem. Jess was holding out hope that the chef would be able to make it in, but it's not safe for anyone to be out like this.

Claire's in the kitchen making something for dinner. I'm sitting near the fireplace, drinking the rest of my cocktail—and I fear I'll never be able to drink another hot toddy in my life without thinking about Claire or this happenstance trip.

Not like I've had many hot toddies before this, but they're pretty damn good.

We offered to cook for Jess and sit down with her but she insisted she had something to do. No clue what that could be, considering there's still no other guests—just me and Claire. She's good at this... sort of moves around you but you barely notice she's there and when she is, she's popping in with some sort of treat or snack.

Claire told me she needed almost an hour for dinner but it would be worth it, so I'm just soaking in the quiet. Maybe dozing off here or there. It's rare for me to have multiple nights like this off in a row, but Willow's schedule has slowed down for the moment. I used to have a bunch of freelance clients, or random events I'd work, but Willow pays me more than I'll ever need in this lifetime and I've been trying to figure out some other things I could do.

Can't be a body guard forever. My muscles ache at the lack of movement the last few days. Even when we were in Miami for the reward show, the event security was on top of it, really making my job easy. I need to do some stretches tonight, maybe a little yoga flow. Wonder if Claire knows any yoga?

Before my mind runs away with all the things that Claire knows, or can do, or can do to me, I hear plates being set on the table in the dining room.

Rounding the corner, I see pasta, salad, and glasses of more bubbly wine. My mouth waters.

"Wow," I say, pulling out the chair, eager to sit down and dig in. "What do we have here?"

Claire beams, the candles making her skin glow. "Fresh pasta with a Parmesan sauce, salad, and Jess showed me where all the wine is and basically made it feel like if we didn't open another bottle we'd be doing her a disservice."

I make a note to leave additional cash in our room when we leave.

"Wait, you made fresh pasta?" I ask, grabbing a fork.

Claire sits and says, "I learned at a cooking class. It's pretty easy and you can definitely taste the difference." She spins some of the noodles around her fork. "I could show you sometime."

The offer of us doing something together, once this is all over, has heat spreading up my neck, to my cheeks. It reminds me of how

Abigail and I would cook together, one of our favorite date night activities. We never got around to making fresh pasta but always wanted to.

"I'd love to learn," I answer before taking a bite. The pasta is perfectly chewy, the Parmesan sauce not too rich, notes of black pepper coming through. I can't help but groan. "Damn, this is ridiculously good," I compliment her.

She smiles and we eat in silence. And it sort of feels just right. I don't know what it is about the two of us, but everything from the flight to the car ride to getting stuck here—none of it has been strained or really all that uncomfortable.

I've been around a while, and this isn't something that happens everyday. The actual events, yes, but the ability to blend in with someone, like you were always meant to.

She clears her throat, a napkin to her mouth, before she says, "Don't take this the wrong way, but—"

My heart drops. There's no way this is going somewhere I want it to. Fitting, considering my brain was like WOW LOOK HOW EASY THIS IS. Just kidding, you idiot.

"I'm not sick of you yet." Claire sits back, smiling at me.

That is not what I thought she'd say.

Her laugh cuts through as she tucks her hair behind her ears. "That sounds bad. But I haven't spent this much time with someone, uninterrupted, in years. Like I honestly can't remember when. And I'm not sick of you yet." She brings the flute of champagne to her lips, taking a slow sip, her eyes golden like a fall sunset.

"I appreciate that." I lock my eyes on hers, wanting her to hear me. "I've not done something like this since Abigail."

The second her name is on my lips, I almost choke. It's been a long time since I've talked about her. To anyone.

"Abigail? Who is that?" Claire follows up with the logical next question.

I take a drink from my own flute, knowing I'm crossing some sort of line, stepping into some unknown area without much place to run from. I buy as much time as isn't awkward and then give her the answer.

"She is... was... my wife."

Twenty-One
Claire

WIFE? HE WAS MARRIED? I did not see that coming.

"Married? I never knew," I reply, the most vague thing that comes to my mind without blowing off the admission.

"Long before I was in the city. When I was a firefighter. Back in Michigan."

Long before.

"Wow, you had like a whole life before this." I think about how one day I could say the same thing about being a manager for someone like Willow in New York, and look back on those days as something completely different from now.

His eyes are looking down, past the plate of food, maybe past the table. His fork taps the bowl. *Tap. Tap. Tap.*

In my gut, I know this story doesn't have a happy ending. This man looked more comfortable when we were making an emergency landing, or even when he was trying to drive on the ice-slicked roads. He was attentive and cautious but there's something different about him now—I can't put my finger on it.

"I did. Feels like a million years ago." He pushes food around his plate, still not looking up.

This feels unfinished. Like, he can't bring up this person and all he shares about her is that she was his wife in Michigan? Maybe I'm prying, maybe I'm not owed any of it, but I ask the question anyway.

I swallow past the hesitancy and ask, "Do you and Abigail still keep in touch?"

His jaw ticks and he sets his fork down so fast, it sort of clangs against the bowl. The silence is heavy for one of the first times, tension growing on the edges of it, like it's a living thing.

"No, it's not like that." He finishes the wine in his glass and looks at me, his face a little pale and quieter than I'm used to. The strong and composed version I've been lucky to know is sort of slipping into something softer.

"When I was a firefighter, there was a snowstorm, not as bad as this one." He looks out the window, tipping his head. "But we got a call. I got there and saw her car. She was in an accident; someone crossed the center line. It wasn't her fault. But she didn't make it." His voice cracks, one that I can hear only because there's literally nothing besides the two of us.

My heart drops to the bottom of whatever depth we exist in. My mouth is dry and I'm looking for words.

"That was almost fifteen years ago. I tried staying in Michigan in the house we bought, the one we planned to stay in until we could build what we wanted. Tried going back to work. But every time we got a call, I'd break down. Panic attacks. Blackouts." The words come out of his mouth like he's reading from a shopping list. Short. Brief. "Took some time off. Tried coming back a second time, and it didn't get better."

I reach out and grab his forearm, squeezing with my fingers. "Seth. I'm sorry." And then all I can think about is how he had to drive us here, on those snowy roads, with the ice hiding beneath the service. He took care of me even though he probably would've rather slept on the floor of the airport.

"It's okay. Long time ago." He tries to shake out his shoulders, like he can move on from the memory of the tragedy if he does it just right. "I thought my whole life was in Michigan, so part of me is thankful I've been able to find other things somewhere, like New York."

"How did you get into this job?" I try to push him past the innate sadness I'm sure must rock him every single day. My hand is still on his forearm and part of me wants to pull him in close to me.

"I had a few connections from the fire department. At first, it started with me working the door at some clubs and bars. There was this specific night where one of my regulars was leaving with her boyfriend. He got aggressive, not even ten feet from the door I was working, and when I stepped in, it was one of the first times I felt like I'd found a part of my way. Like, I could still keep people safe."

My eyes are wide and my heart is bursting—this man is truly something else in the best way. I don't know everything about Seth but I know he loves to watch out for others. It's key to him as a person, and that's probably why he's damn good at being Willow's head of security.

"That's actually pretty amazing. Think about all the good you've done. The people you've kept safe."

His eyes drift and he doesn't even have to say it. *He couldn't keep her safe.*

"Maybe," he suggests, his mind elsewhere.

It hurts to watch him like this, going through the internal boxing match he does probably more than he'd ever admit to.

"You kept me safe. And you absolutely didn't have to. We were just going to the same place. Thank you for that."

"It's nothing. Don't worry about it." A corner of his mouth tries to pull up.

I squeeze his arm harder and his eyes fall to mine as I say, "It's something to me."

Twenty-Two

Seth

I HAD NO INTENTION of telling Claire about Abigail tonight, but that's where we ended up. It's hard to think about how long I've lived without her, the life she didn't get. One of the other reasons I ended up in New York was that it was one of her favorite places. We'd taken a few vacations and tried to fit in as many restaurants as we could in a short amount of time—she was a foodie.

I do love the idea of being happy in the place she loved so much. I'm not sure about the afterlife or what happens when we die, but part of me holds hope that she knows where I'm at, what I'm doing, and it doesn't feel like I wasted the precious time I had.

A lot of people in New York don't know I was married. It really does feel like I cut my life like a piece of rope, and tied it off. Then, I started a new one in a different state. Every once in a while, I go back to the old rope, all the things hanging from it, but they stay put after. Even if they wanted to come to New York, I always go back to them, not wanting to mix things up.

We're rinsing dishes in the kitchen, the warm water rinsing the bubbles from the plates. I insisted on doing the dishes, since Claire cooked, but she was adamant we do it together. We make quick work of it, Claire drying the last of the dishes and putting them away.

She turns and faces me, hands on her hips, scanning for anything else for us to do in the back-to-immaculate kitchen—every counter wiped and everything spotless.

Slowly, she steps closer to me. She doesn't say anything but instead wraps her arms around me, resting her head on my chest.

I hug her back and we sway back and forth for a few seconds. I knew it was the right thing to share with her, tell her about one of the pieces of me that's rare to find, and she couldn't have been nicer to me. There was no toxic positivity or bullshit take on how she's in a better place or anything like that. It felt like everything I said...just was.

"I mean it. Thank you for taking care of me. And for making my birthday one to remember."

She melts into me and her weight is like the weighted blanket my therapist told me about, the one I use when things get dark. The one that makes me feel like I can claw myself out of whatever hole I'm in.

"Could've done without the emergency landing, but, you're welcome." I hold her to me and feel her shake with a laugh. My own lips pull into what feels like a smile. And I don't say it, but I feel it.

This means something to me, too.

The Fable Inn is mostly modern, but then Jess tells us about the hot water bottles she put in our room while we were having dinner and it makes me question my judgement. I've never come into contact with one until tonight, but it gets a ten out of ten for me. Even though she turned the generator on, the wind has picked up outside. It might be barely snowing, but you can't see a thing. Plus, the wind is so shrill, it whistles as it creeps through parts of the window, making the room cooler than last night.

We're under the blankets, Claire's laptop balanced on her lap with enough battery for us to watch another movie—we'll need to charge it tomorrow.

"Is now a bad time to tell you that the only thing I have downloaded are all of the Scream movies?" She puts a hand over her mouth, probably covering a laugh.

"Put the next one on," I insist as she taps the keys. "I can't tell you how long it's been since I saw the second one."

When she settles in, she curls into me, resting her head on my chest. Maybe we need to stick together for warmth or maybe this is just the pull. The place we end up. Either way, I'm not complaining.

Before we get too far into the movie, I pull out my phone, checking the weather for tomorrow. I hold the screen in a way that both of us can see it as I click the radar and forecast.

"Maybe it will finally stop snowing tomorrow?" Claire says wistfully, as the massive blue blob of winter seems to shrink and disappear while we watch the twenty-four hour radar loop.

"Maybe? I am looking forward to wearing appropriate clothing, not things from my Florida suit case."

She turns, looking up at me, eyes wide and gushes, "Same." She laughs considering she's wearing a T-shirt of hers over the lacy lingerie from last night.

Next, we check the temperature forecast, which shows a significant warm up over the next few days. Like, it's supposed to be 65 in six days. Talk about a swing.

"No icy roads this time next week," she says. "That doesn't compute in my brain. Stuck in a blizzard but back to the pumpkin patches and no winter coats in a week."

"Definitely something I didn't see coming. But, hey, we wouldn't be in a bed with hot water bottles, watching the masterpiece that is Scream 2, if the weather behaved? Right?" I joke and shrug my shoulders, feeling her laugh into me.

Picking her head up, she wags a finger at me. "Don't talk that way about my favorite movie franchise."

"I would never," I tease her, rolling my eyes, and then looking at the laptop screen.

We watch all of the movie, some of the jump-scares getting me, and Claire letting out a laugh I'd pay to listen to when my depression is pulling at me. An honest belly laugh from someone who people legit won't sit next to in meetings because they're scared of her. I love the contrast.

When the movie ends, I hurry out of bed, closing it and putting it on the small table in our room. Climbing back into bed, Claire is waiting for me to get comfortable.

Last night, I couldn't help but think of touching her. Tasting her. Making her moan. But tonight? The thought of us just being here with each other is enough.

Twenty-Three
Claire

THE DOOR OPENS AND it wakes me up. My eyes catch Seth walking in, holding something. I reach my arms and stretch my muscles, the room much warmer than last night. Plus, the personal heater known as Seth definitely made me more comfortable.

"Morning. I know you're looking for caffeine, but I knew there were fresh oranges. So, how about mimosas?" He asks while holding the wine from the chiller—almost a full bottle from dinner.

A cappuccino may be my drink of choice, but a mimosa is a close second. "I'll allow it," I say, getting out of bed and taking care of myself in the bathroom.

I'm washing my hands after brushing my teeth, and I pause when I see my reflection. My skin looks like it's glowing, the break from wearing makeup has been kind of nice. I'm the kind of person who wears makeup because I love doing it, but it's not something I've missed the last few days. Also, the way Seth looked at me? Made me feel better than any night I'd been out with a full face of makeup on.

I use my travel size bottle of moisturizer, following one of the morning routines I'm thankful I've been able to keep on this weird trip. Opening the container that holds my pills when I travel, I take my last Prozac and a little jolt of worry hits me. I always bring a few extra, but after this, maybe I start carrying a full week's worth.

Walking out, I hold the teal and blue capsule, looking for my water bottle. Now, I'd be lying if I said I'd never taken my med with a mimosa but having a swig of water feels like a better start. It's about balance—one of the best things a therapist has ever told me.

"I'd like to try and get home because this is my last one," I say, tossing it in my mouth, and chasing it with some water.

"What is it?" Seth asks, pouring fresh orange juice in the flutes.

"I'm a member of the Prozac club." I put my hand up, trying to show him that it doesn't bother me to talk about.

"You should be okay if you miss one. Or if it's late. It's a delayed release." He pours the bubbly into the glass and again, he surprises me. When I don't say anything, but my eyebrows push into my forehead, he continues. "I was part of the same club for a few years." He offers me a flute, smiling.

"I swear, you're unlike any man I've ever met." I lift my drink and he clinks his glass to mine.

Therapy. Meds. Coping mechanisms. Seth seems to be a walking green flag—and it's greener because he put the work in.

"I did plug in your laptop and your charging bank while we have power. Chatted with Jess this morning and she says the generators are off and the power's on for now."

I take a drink, the mimosa a perfect blend of the sweet, fresh citrus and the sharp bubbles. I'm afraid I'm going to give this man a complex with too many compliments.

"And we can do some laundry. I figure we could at least wash the crew necks we lived in yesterday, with anything else that could be washed together." He suggests something so simple, yet why is it that I'm turned on as this man talks about laundry?

Seth zips open his suitcase and starts pulling out the things he'd like to wash. When he pulls out a tie, he hangs it on the back of a chair. I'm painfully aware that I'm still wearing my lingerie, a black shirt over it, but my nipples tingle like they're itching to be touched.

He looks up at me, just for a second, before standing with his hands on his hips. "What's that look for?"

Oh, you know, just turned on by you talking about laundry. Or wearing a tie. Or using a tie. These are the thoughts I have but refuse to share. Instead, I say, "No look."

I do my best to keep my face as normal as possible, taking another drink.

"Your cheeks are all pink. What is it?" He tries to coax the answer.

Trying to laugh it off, my eyes fall on the tie, for just a second, and he clocks it. His eyes land on the tie, before he crosses his arms and looks at me.

"Ohhhh. Okay. It's the tie." He picks up the fabric, wearing a smirk that's making me wet, and runs it through his fingers. The tie is black satin and I know it's soft in his hands.

I set the flute down and say, "It's only a tie. And, no look." I wave a hand in front of my face before crossing my arms.

He walks closer, knowing I'm not telling the truth, wearing that greedy smirk. My legs want to buckle, get down in front of him, but I force myself to stand.

"What could I do with this tie?" he questions, but sounds like it's only for him to think about. "I could tie your hands together. Use the frame of the bed. Not let you touch anything." He's in front of me, pulling the tie around my shoulders—my arms still crossed.

He takes one of the ends and rubs it along my jaw, before putting his fingers under my chin and tipping my face up to his.

"Or I could blindfold you." His words fall down my skin, and my breasts are heavy, knowing he's only a lean away.

I can't help but bite my lip at the suggestion. Because I want all of it.

"You just gave yourself away. Biting that lip." His mouth is close to mine and before I can argue, or lie and tell him he's wrong, he puts a full kiss to my mouth. He tastes me and I open for him, wanting him to take all that he wants. Give me all I need.

"Turn." Seth's voice is rough and pointed.

There's nothing to do but follow directions. So I turn, my ass pushing into his hips. The tie comes up and he places it over my eyes, tying it behind my head. The thick fabric steals my vision and there's a sort of thrill of not being able to see what happens next.

My awareness for Seth is through the roof. It's like all of the details, every clue, is amplified. When he finally stops moving around me, his lips find my ear lobe, nipping it as he growls, "Arms. Up."

I lift my arms and Seth grabs the bottom of my lingerie. Slowly, he pulls it up over my head, each inch of my skin becoming bare to him. The only thing left on my body is his tie and my black lacy thong.

I hear the sound of him folding my clothes, most likely setting them somewhere, but I don't move. When I feel him close to me, I itch to wrap my arms around him, pull him closer.

I shiver when I feel his finger tips graze the side of my ass to the front of my hip. He pushes his length against me and it takes everything I have to not bend over and ask him to fuck me.

"You've got a thing for lace, huh? You probably like the way it rubs on your skin." He takes a hand, and rubs down my center, over the fabric.

I answer with a simple, "Yes." My knees want to wobble and fail me but I lean backwards into him, giving a little more access to my front.

"Are these panties dry? Tell me what I'll find if I check."

He emphasizes the word "if" and I bite back a moan. I can't imagine him not touching me.

"They're wet." My words are clipped and have me begging for breath.

"Are you soaking through for me, baby?" he croons. "Tell me."

I swallow past the needy lump in my throat and do my best to answer. "Yes. I know I'm—soaking wet. Waiting for you."

"You think you can be patient?" His words are quick to meet my answer.

"Yes," I lie.

"Let's get you on the bed," he says while guiding me. The front of my legs hit the mattress, then he turns me and pushes me back.

Suddenly he's gone. I feel him moving around the room; hear him, but he's not touching me. I'm aching for him; even though I said I could be patient, I don't know if I can.

My stomach contracts at his absence, the burning in my core scorching—that's what he does to me.

"Scoot back," he says. I move until my head hits the pillow.

I feel him press into the bed, hear the sounds of the mattress giving way. He carefully hooks a pinky at my entrance, feeling my panties for himself.

"Oh, Claire. I think we can do better than this."

I expect him to take my panties off. Touch me with his fingers. His mouth.

Instead, it's a jolt that I've never felt before. One which sends my shoulders up and off the pillows, leaning forward, before falling back into the bed.

It's something cold, wet, leaving a trail as he moves it up the inside of my thigh.

An ice cube.

Seth moves up my body, the ice in his fingers, away from my skin. He takes a nipple in his mouth, nipping it, rolling his tongue. The warmth of his lips is quickly replaced with the ice cube and a whine falls from my mouth. Part of me wants to pull the blindfold off, watch him tease me with fire and ice, and the other wants me to beg him to keep going.

Moving to my other breast, he starts with the ice, swirling it on my skin until it's almost numb. Over and over. He licks around the ice cube, lapping up the wetness. The soothing of his mouth, followed by the chill of the ice, is inching me closer and closer.

Then he's gone. His mouth. The ice cube. Nowhere to be found. My panting breath fills the space, and just when I'm about to ask where he went, he puts the ice cube on my clit.

Twenty-Four

Seth

Claire gasps when I lightly press the ice cube to her clit, melting through the lace. I feel her muscles pull in and it's the kind of encouragement that makes me never want to stop. She keeps pushing her full bottom lip through her teeth as her hands grip the sheets.

Fuck. She's gorgeous like this.

I'm obsessed with watching the ice melt. Dripping down to the bedding, glistening on her skin, burning my fingers with the grip I refuse to relent.

My dick is hard and is throbbing with each second that goes on. I'll be painting my shorts if I don't watch it.

I move the cube up to the waistband of her panties then back down. Claire moans when the ice is on her clit again. Her black panties outline the curves of her hips, her ass, and I love seeing her in lace.

"Told you we could do better," I tease, feeling her entrance with my finger, the one without the ice cube. "We could ring these out, baby." I say, pleased with her reaction.

I take the ice and move it on the inside of her thigh, watching her shiver. My lips kiss up the same trail until my lips graze the lacy band of her panties pulling across the front of her hip.

My fingers grab her panties and pull them down all the way to her ankles, off her feet, and then toss them on the floor.

"Spread those legs. Now." I urge her to give me the view I've been dreaming about.

And the good listener that she is, Claire pulls her knees apart, letting them rest on the bed. I lick my lips, needing to taste her.

Carefully, I hold the ice in between my index and middle finger and slowly insert it in her entrance. Before she can decipher what's happening, I put my lips near my finger, licking her up.

And then she's begging me and saying my name, over and over, like a prayer.

I give her what she wants, slowly pumping my fingers inside her, the ice mixing with her wetness, as my mouth works her. At first, I match the pace of my fingers with my tongue, slow and steady, pressing against her. But when I switch it up, my tongue flicking fast, she can't take it and reaches for my head.

I let her pull my hair and put my mouth where she wants it, where her hands direct me.

"Seth!" Her voice is desperate and I know she's about to unravel.

The ice cube is almost all the way melted and her muscles are starting to clench on my fingers. I moan into her, the extra vibrations all she needs to completely fall off the ledge. Her climax hits her hard, a yell coming from her mouth that catches me off guard, but I don't stop. I keep eating her even when she's trying to roll away from me, trying to take a break.

But I'm not done with her yet.

My mouth stays on her until she's spent and laying in a heap on the bed. She's pulled off the tie covering her eyes and the way she looks at me—it's something I want to remember forever. Something I won't be able to forget.

While she's collecting herself, I move the full length mirror that's in the corner of the room. I put one of the sitting chairs in front of it. I walk to the side of the bed, my cock pulsing against the fabric of my shorts, and offer Claire a hand.

"Come here," I plead. She doesn't hesitate, giving me one of her hands and getting off the bed. This time, I have no intention of covering her eyes—she's going to watch all of this. Instead, I put her in front of the chair. I take the tie and lightly knot it behind her head, but this time the satin fabric is in her mouth, in between her teeth. Her skin is creamy, but red in spots from the ice cube, and it's like a maze of pleasure running over parts of her body.

"Okay?" I check that she's still on the same page and she emphatically nods her head. My fucking good girl.

"Look," I gesture to the mirror. Pointing to a spot of wetness on the front of my pants, they're dark from my precum. "See what you do to me?" And I swear she melts into the chair, her arms holding her up.

My hands push into the backs of her thighs, up her ass, and I spank one side as I growl, "Bend. Over."

Claire groans into the tie, her sound muffled, but she reaches for the edge of the chair, arching her back and putting her ass on full display for me. I dip into her wetness and coat my fingers with it, then lightly press a finger on her tight hole, one I've not claimed yet. I circle the skin, letting her unclench and relax, and when I look to the mirror, she's watching me.

Her hips wiggle, chasing the pressure of my finger when I pull it away. She wants it. And that makes me almost come unglued. The site of me using her wetness to lube her ass is about ready to send me to another planet.

I knead one ass cheek while still gently pressing with the other hand. "Okay?" I ask, making sure to keep her comfortable and also because I love hearing her. Watching her agree to however I want to touch her. Take her. Fuck her. There's no way I could fuck her the way I want to without some prep work, but we'll take what we can with ass play.

"Yes. Please," she begs, voice sort of covered with the tie in her mouth. Her back arches deeper and she stretches her chin up.

"Such a good girl," I groan. Carefully I put in a finger, only making it to my middle knuckle before she's whimpering underneath me. I twirl and push the finger into different parts of her, letting her feel all of it. When I take it out, Claire whines for me, my name muffled. Again, I push in, maybe a little further but still playing it safe. When I pull it out, my other hand grabs my cock and guides it to her pussy.

"Push into me, baby," I insist with my cock barely in her.

Her hands grip the chair and she pushes her hips back to me, letting me fill her inch by inch. She leans forward, and then takes more of me. I watch as she soaks my length, and when she finds a rhythm, I spank her ass again.

"Now, it's my turn. From here on out, you hold onto the chair and you watch. Got it?"

Her head nods and I swear she fucking smiles at me.

Fuck. I'm already close.

One of my hands grips her thigh while the other waits at her other hole, the one I'm going to finger fuck. I set the pace, watching her in the mirror.

My voice is like gravel when I call out, "This greedy cunt is going to milk me, isn't it?" I bury my cock inside her and she takes all of me, like I knew she could.

"Yes!" Claire yells and I can feel her core getting tight, knowing she's going to come for me again.

I keep thrusting inside her and put a finger in her ass. I'm careful not to get carried away with it and instead take it out on her pussy, which I know she can handle. The finger presses and moves pressure as I thrust my dick harder.

The sounds of her about to cry out match her face, and I fuck her faster and deeper. She starts to reach for shallow breaths and I watch her lock into her reflection in the mirror—her knuckles white from holding on. I watch as she finds her second climax and when her walls strangle my dick, I quickly spill my cum into her. I don't stop fucking her, even when she's laying on the chair, her arms not holding her up anymore. Even with her head turned to the side, she keeps watching what she can.

I come inside Claire and feel her moan through it, the vibrations somehow reaching the head of my cock, as the shocks slow. I bend forward, placing a kiss on her back, and I feel her giggle against me.

"Stay here," I say, gentler than before, and go start the shower.

I come back and she hasn't moved. My hands pull the tie from her mouth and I stand her up, turning to face me. And the fucking smile she's wearing cracks my chest open.

Her hands loop around my neck, part of her needing some assistance standing, and she gives me a full kiss on the lips—smirking into it.

She pulls away, eyes golden with satisfaction, and she almost whispers, "This might be the best birthday weekend ever."

I kiss her back, letting the compliment wash over me, before walking us back. "Let's get you cleaned up."

We're under the stream of hot water in under a minute and we simply stand together. I rub my fingers along her back as she rests her head on my chest. She sighs and even lets out a little laugh. And the way she makes me feel catches me off guard.

Like, she lets me take control—be rough—but she's just as eager to share this slow moment in the shower after. It's complex. It's honest. And it's something I haven't been able to feel in a long time.

And that's everything.

TWENTY-FIVE

Claire

I FEEL LIKE A new person. Now, one could attribute that to the trauma response of the last few days, plus some mind-bending orgasms, and my morning full of rough sex, a sweet shower, and then a two hour nap.

Seth took care of me in the shower, even washing my hair, and I don't know if that's ever happened before. Have I ever been with a man who can tie me up one minute and then carefully lather shampoo for me in the next? No. Don't think I have. *I've been missing out.*

We woke up from our nap, which felt ridiculous at first considering we had just gotten up, but my bones were happily exhausted. Then we had our mimosas in bed. Seth even went and put a load of our laundry in the washer.

I've just been hanging out in bed when Seth comes upstairs, offering me clothes warm from the dryer. Another small act of kindness but one that screams volumes. Looking at my phone, I see that it's almost noon, and I need to get up and move.

I change into a clean pair of biker shorts, the Fable Inn crewneck, and a pair of Seth's socks. Everything is fresh from the laundry and somehow feels cozier than before. My hair has air dried into a bigger-than-I'd-typically-let-anyone-see wave situation, but it feels good to be in new clothes.

I pull back the curtains to the window and the sun is out in full force. Everything is blanketed in white, making the sun brighter than normal. Snow is barely falling and it feels like the end is in reach. I take a long, slow breath, letting it expand in my chest, before sighing it out. This went way better than I thought it would—being stuck here—and that's all because of Seth. Well, some credit is due to The Fable Inn, and Jess—this was a gem of an accommodation to stumble on.

"I really like it here," Seth shares, like he's reading my mind. He's wearing the same crewneck, all fresh and laundered, and the jogger pants he also washed.

"Me too. I bet it's gorgeous during the *actual* fall." I cross my arms and look back out the window. The trees sport autumn leaves covered in snow and I hope they'll be able to bounce back. Fall is the best season and it'd be a shame to cut it short.

Seth comes up behind me, also peeking out the window. "Well, we could come back. On purpose."

I turn to him, being met with his strong chest, and he's looking at me all matter of fact and like he's suggesting we get lunch next week. When I don't say anything, he continues, "If you're interested."

This is one of the only times we've acknowledged what comes after this. What do you do when you give in for a handful of days, and then plan to go back to your old life soon? Soon it will be schedules, my apartment, and us sharing a client.

I'd be lying if I said I wasn't interested.

"I think that'd be fun." I smile at him as he gives me a soft peck on my forehead.

Out of all the places he's kissed me, this one makes me pause. It's so intimate and sweet. I quiet the alarm bell that's trying to ding in my brain, the one that tells me not to read too much into it.

Seth is nothing like what I would've expected. I have no idea where this is going— maybe we'll get in the car and leave this all behind or maybe there's something waiting for us in the city. Either way, I'm willing to be as patient as my type-A personality will allow.

His hands rub my shoulders and says, "I need coffee... which means you're probably way overdue." He laughs at my mild caffeine addiction. "Let's go downstairs and hang for a bit."

Seth grabs my hand and leads me out the door, and he doesn't let go until he needs both hands to make my cappuccino. I fall into one of the oversized chairs in front of the roaring fireplace. The lights are on and the inn has a different type of cozy energy; things are buzzing and sighing that were missing without the power over the last few nights.

Jess sees me and beams, sitting next to me. "Looks like you'll be able to get out of here tonight or tomorrow. The snow is letting up and it's already starting to melt. It'll be back to our October rain in no time."

"Thank you for everything while we were stuck here. Honestly, it was lovely," I say to her as a song comes on in the room, one I know well—one by Willow.

Jess nods and immediately starts singing along to herself.

"You like this one?" I ask, sort of baiting her.

"Who doesn't? Plus, Willow and Tripp, they're easy to root for."

I smile at the compliment she gives my client, my friend. I've been working with Willow for a long time. She was the first name who really took a chance on me, and she got big quick. Not only is she talented, but she's one of the kindest souls I've ever met.

"Well, if you promise to keep it between us, I'm her manager. I'd love to get your information and the next time she's on tour, we'll make sure you get tickets. On me." I place a hand on my chest.

"You do not have to do that." She tries to turn down the offer and she's about to stand, probably to run and get some sort of snack tray or something for Seth and me.

Lightly, I put my hand on hers that's resting on the arm of the chair, "I know I don't have to, but I'd be thrilled to do it."

She smiles at me in a way that's true. "Okay, if you insist." I grin at her as she walks back through the inn, passing Seth with two coffee cups.

"Cappuccinos for two," he announces, sitting next to me. I take the mug from him and take a sip, the espresso and milk perfectly balanced—the foam velvety on my lips.

"What now?" I ask, knowing I'm going to need another one of these.

He takes a sip from his own mug and gestures to the TV, "Well, we should see what other terrible things are in store for Sidney Prescott in the next Scream movie. Right?"

The fact that he's clocked into these details of my favorite spooky movie franchise has me shaking my head in awe. "Are you sure? We can watch something else if you want."

"No, let's get to the rest of these movies." He stands, finding the remote and pulling up a streaming service. "Looks like we're running out of time." Seth cranes his neck to look out the window, watching the snow melt off the trees. "We should be able to head home tomorrow. Want to look for a flight?"

"What if we drove back? Had a little road trip instead? As long as the roads are okay?" I'm quiet in my suggestion and know that asking Seth to drive that far back instead of taking a quick flight is quite the move.

He tilts his head, shoulders dropping a bit, and answers, "What, you're not sick of me yet?" One corner of his mouth tugs up.

"Not even close," I say, slow and honest.

And I mean it.

TWENTY-SIX
Seth

DID YOU KNOW THAT there are currently seven Scream movies? I thought we were talking about a basic trilogy, but this franchise went hard. So, that's what we've done all day. Cuddled up in our chairs, or the love seat, or on the floor, covered with a freshly washed comforter—courtesy of Jess.

I can't tell you the last time I've laughed this hard or been so invested in a string of movies. Mostly, I love how Claire loves them. Sometimes, people are afraid to jump into something head first because they're afraid of how it will look—it could never be Claire.

Maybe that's it? She's confident in what she wants, what she needs, what she likes. It's the whole drinking hot coffee, no matter the temperature, and watching her favorite movie franchise multiple times throughout the year. She knows what she wants and also how to get it, if we're being honest.

We're eating our second bowl of popcorn—our fingers all buttery and salty. Jess saw our movie marathon and didn't quit bringing us food, snacks, and then lunch. She even made some cocktails, including a pair of espresso martinis. I may have shown her how to use the espresso machine, the one she had no reason to be intimidated by.

The martini is probably why we're still wide eyed and awake at almost midnight. It's like she knew we needed more time together, like this, in our own little world. Our last movie is going through all the plot twists and revelations and we've got to be close to the end.

I check the weather a final time and see that we'll be in great shape to make the drive tomorrow. When Claire suggested we drive, instead of fly, my stomach flipped in a way that reminded me of those early interactions with someone you care about. Logistically, it would be easier. I'm sure the airport will be a nightmare tomorrow, considering a few days of grounded flights and chaos.

So, we'll drive the eight hours, and really stretch out the end of the trip. I already checked with Jess and she has some to-go cups for coffee and is going to send us with a snack basket—she promised the homemade peanut butter and jelly sandwiches and my mouth is watering thinking about it.

I look over to Claire, her feet resting in my lap as we sit on the floor. One hand is in the popcorn bowl, bringing it to her smiling mouth, as she watches the end of one of her favorite movies—even though the seventh one isn't her favorite, a distinction she made several times. Her face is bright from the TV, and lips are a little pink from the salt, and probably the kissing we did earlier.

This moment feels significant. I've struggled with thinking about the universe, or karma, or whatever you believe in–losing Abigail made it impossible. But now, this whole wild thing feels more like a gift than anything else. I know I'm grinning to myself as we see the next Ghostface reveal and I don't care.

Fuck. This was quite the surprise. Glad I thought about a rule, something I guessed she'd buy into, knowing how methodical and planned of a person she is. A fleeting thought that brought one of my favorite few days in a very long time.

The one bed rule.

Our rule.

And I hold on to that during our last night at The Fable Inn.

TWENTY-SEVEN

Claire

AFTER ALMOST NINE HOURS of driving, dropping off the rental car, and taking a car into the city, we're in front of my apartment. I should be tired, sick of being in the car, but I'm not. I'd do it all over again, just like this. Just like our time at The Fable Inn, the drive was fairly easy and much more enjoyable when we weren't white knuckling it like when we left the airport earlier this week.

"I'll walk you up," Seth says, getting out of the car and grabbing our bags from the trunk. He didn't want to make the driver wait, so he said he'd call another car. Honestly, the man is too thoughtful.

The familiar routine of typing in my code in the keypad to unlock the door has me excited to be home. The Fable Inn was perfect for what we needed, and even though I do plan to visit again, I'm so happy to be home. I'm thinking about my favorite coffee shop, the weekend bagel I missed out on from my favorite bakery, and just the buzz of the city I love so much.

Seth is close behind as we get into the elevator, taking me to my floor. We don't do the small talk thing, but instead soak in the silence. It feels comfortable. Warm.

The doors open and Seth gestures for me to walk out first. I lead him to the door, put my key in and open it. The smell is familiar and one that makes me even more happy to be home. Seth sets my bag down and stands with his hands on his hips.

"Well, glad to see we made it back in one piece," he jokes.

"Yes, it's good to be home." I stand in my doorway, looking back inside to my place.

A hand pushes through his salt-and-pepper hair, and his jaw ticks as his eyes fall on mine. Fuck, that look will never get old.

"Between you and me, sort of glad we didn't get back on an airplane." He puts a hand on his chest. "It's too soon."

"Me too," I say; one, because the emergency landing will be a hard one to shake, and second, because we were able to spend more time together.

"Alright, well I'm going to head out." Seth points back down the hallway to the elevator.

I shift my weight to one foot and tilt my head, taking him in from head to toe. I've thought about this moment ever since I suggested the drive back. During the drive, I kept reminding myself how this was a blip in our timeline. Nothing that was planned–just the universe bringing us together.

I'd be content if our time together was just what it was, at The Fable Inn, and nowhere else. But, I'd never forgive myself if I didn't go for what I wanted.

"Hey," I grab his forearm as he turns to leave, "Do you want to come in?"

His face breaks into a grin, the one that makes me want to kiss him. Right then and there. Like we've been doing it forever.

Seth nods, still wearing that smile that is contagious, grabbing the bags and steps in my apartment. I close the door and feel like my heartbeat is echoing off the walls—quick and nervous. When Seth walks in, he leaves the bags on the floor by my coffee table, and he takes a scan of the room. My place is always tidy and put together–I'm someone driven by lists and getting things done.

"How many bedrooms?" he asks about my apartment, peeking down the hall.

"Two. But one is an office" I answer.

Seth closes the distance between us and grabs me, pulling me in for a kiss. He breaks it long enough to say, "So, you're telling me there's only one bed?"

And he picks me up, kissing me like he means it. I laugh into it because if there's one thing about me, it's that I love to follow a rule.

THE END

Looking for more Seth and Claire? Scan the QR code for the BONUS EPILOGUE

Acknowledgments

This is one of those projects that wouldn't have been possible without readers, my author friends, and just people in general taking a chance on me. I didn't publicly announce this book until a week prior to release. The typical lead time for a book was thrown out the window and I did something completely different.

Without my author friends who kept telling me to keep going, that people would bite on the idea of something secret, and my secret reader group who proved them right, this book wouldn't be in your hands right now.

To the readers who were invited to the project, by myself, or one of my VIP readers, THANK YOU. Thank you for saying yes, taking a chance...on something you had no idea what it was, and even joining a random Facebook group to play along. I had so much fun with this and couldn't have done it without you all.

To my alpha readers, Stephanie and Rose, thanks for taking on another one of my wild ideas and helping me get it to the finish line. To my editor, Kendra, thank you for adding this to your roster out of basically nowhere and helping me make it the best it could be.

I love you. Thank you for reading.

RACHEL LABERGE is the author of THE ONE BED RULE. She's known for writing love stories where the characters' brains are spicy... just like the plot.

You can connect with her on Instagram, TikTok, and Threads **@rachellabergeauthor** (no 'R' name required).

Scan the QR code to join Rachel's newsletter and be first in line for announcements, PR opportunities, and more!